KENSY AND MAX

DISAPPEARING ACT

Kensy and Max Books

Jacqueline Harvey

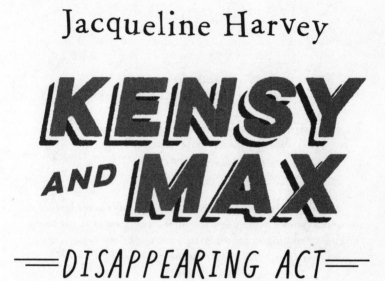

KENSY
AND MAX

=DISAPPEARING ACT=

Kane Miller
A DIVISION OF EDC PUBLISHING

First American Edition 2020
Kane Miller, A Division of EDC Publishing

First published Random House Australia in 2018,
Penguin Random House Australia Pty Ltd.
Copyright © Jacqueline Harvey 2018
The moral right of the author has been asserted.

For information contact:
Kane Miller, A Division of EDC Publishing
P.O. Box 470663
Tulsa, OK 74147-0663
www.kanemiller.com
www.edcpub.com
www.usbornebooksandmore.com

Library of Congress Control Number: 2019940411

Printed and bound in the United States of America
1 2 3 4 5 6 7 8 9 10
ISBN: 978-1-61067-993-0

For Ian, my best friend and biggest fan, and for Holly and Catriona, who believed in Kensy and Max right from the start and have worked so hard to help me bring them to life

Lighthouse

Family Crypt

Racetrack

Maze

Greenhouse

Stables

Helipad

Archery
Field

Village

River

Map of
Alexandria

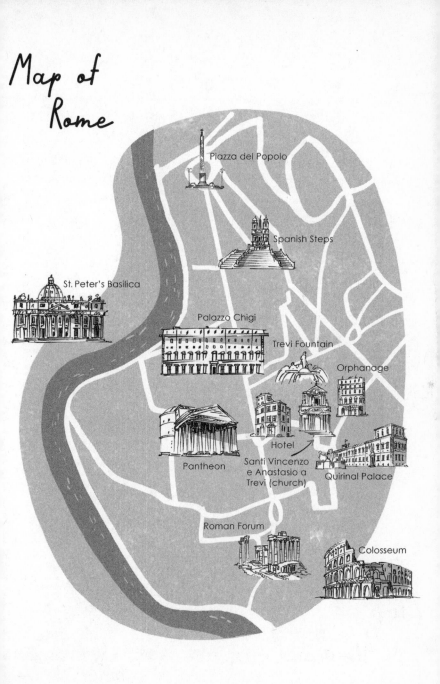

Map of
Rome

Piazza del Popolo

Spanish Steps

St. Peter's Basilica

Palazzo Chigi

Trevi Fountain

Orphanage

Pantheon

Hotel

Santi Vincenzo
e Anastasio a
Trevi (church)

Quirinal Palace

Roman Forum

Colosseum

CAST OF CHARACTERS

The Grey household

Kensington Méribel Grey	11-year-old twin
Maxim Val d'Isère Grey	11-year-old twin
Anna Grey	Kensy and Max's mother
Edward Grey	Kensy and Max's father
Fitzgerald Williams	Kensy and Max's manny, first cousin of Edward Grey

Alexandria Estate

Dame Cordelia Spencer	Head of Pharos
Rupert Spencer	Dame Spencer's younger son
Song	Butler
Mim	Head gardener and Fitz's mother

Shugs	Gardener
Mr. O'Leary	Gardener
Ida Thornthwaite	Cook
Wellington and Mackintosh	Dame Spencer's West Highland terriers

Central London Free School staff

Magoo MacGregor	Headmaster
Romilly Vanden Boom	Science teacher
Monty Reffell	History teacher
Willow Witherbee	English teacher
Elliot Frizzle	Art teacher
Lottie Ziegler	Mathematics teacher
Gordon Nutting	PE teacher
Elva Trimm	Head dinner lady

Central London Free School students

| Autumn Lee, Harper Ballantine, Carlos Rodriguez, Sachin Varma, Yasmina Ahmed, Dante Moretti, Inez Dufour, Misha Thornhill, Alfie Dingle | Kensy and Max's friends |
| Lola Lemmler | School bully |

| Graham Churchill, Harriet, Liam and Winston | History tour participants |

Other

Esmerelda	Driving instructor
Nico	Missing boy
Sidney	Butler
Sister Maria Regina	Nun
Vittoria Vitale	Prime minister of Italy
Lorenzo Rinaldi	Prime minister's husband

GLOSSARY OF ITALIAN TERMS

Allontanatevi dai bambini!	Get away from the children!
borseggiatori	pickpockets
Buon Natale	Merry Christmas
carabinieri	military police
ciao	hello/goodbye
codardo	coward
Cosa avete portato?	What did you bring?
Cosa fai?	What are you doing?
derubato	robbed
diavolo	devil
grazie	thank you
ho vinto	I won
Inglese	English
Italiano	Italian

lei firmerà i documenti	she will sign the documents
mamma mia	an expression of surprise
mi scusi	excuse me
mia cara	my dear
ottimo lavoro	good job
poliziotti	police
Primo Ministro	Prime Minister
scomparso	missing
scusi	sorry
sei morto	you're dead
sì	yes
signora	madam
signore	mister
stupido	stupid
toilette	toilet

Case Note 16

Author: Fitzgerald Williams,
Pharos Agent (PA) S2660
Subjects: Kensington Grey, PA A2713;
Maxim Grey, PA A2714

Kensington and Maxim Grey were admitted as Pharos agents-in-training at the age of eleven years and one month.

FIELDWORK

Via their keen observation and deductive skills, the twins solved the theft of the Graff Peacock Brooch from the Tate Gallery in London, which was perpetrated by Esme Brightside; Wanda Grigsby; Wanda's son, Derek Grigsby; and Ivy Daggett. The foursome had been under the surveillance of MI6 agents for some time following the disappearance of Esme, Wanda and Ivy's husbands, who, eighteen months previously, had pulled off the largest diamond heist in British history. The apprehension of the thieves was undertaken by MI6. However, had it not been for Kensington and Maxim, they would have been outsmarted by the gang, who were caught at the last minute while en route to the Dominican Republic. All four suspects are now in custody awaiting trial. Garnet Brightside, Walter Grigsby and Ray Daggett have also been apprehended and are awaiting extradition from the United States. Kensington and Maxim have received no formal recognition for their efforts, although a large box of chocolates did arrive at Ponsonby Terrace for the children along with a thank-you card from Claudia, the MI6 agent in charge of the investigation.

SKILLS, STRENGTHS AND VULNERABILITIES

Since the disappearance of their parents and subsequent relocation to London, the twins have kept up their physical fitness. Maxim has delved further into code breaking, having recently spent time studying the Caesar cipher. His talent is exceptional. The boy also has a photographic memory, particularly for maps. He must learn to trust his instincts as there will be many occasions in the future where he will need to make quick decisions. While both twins' understanding of Morse code has been tested with good outcomes, Kensington requires further revision and training in this area. She must also remember to wear her watch each day. Her ability to pick locks has proven excellent and will require increasingly difficult devices to expand her knowledge. They both need to work on their disguise recognition and environmental awareness.

TRAINING

The children entered formal training on 17 November and have adapted well to their new schedules. Their ability to conceal their extracurricular activities from the regular students at Central London Free School has thus far been very successful and they have both made good friends within the unit. Kensington's propensity to speak before she thinks has at times landed her in hot water – particularly around Misha, another trainee agent currently on assignment and acting as the close friend of Lola Lemmler, a classmate whose father is of great interest to the organization.

EMOTIONAL STATE

Kensington has exhibited signs of emotional withdrawal, but she has proven incredibly resilient in the face of enormous change and shocking revelations. Maxim has been a steady influence on his sister and, all things considered, they have both adjusted admirably to their unusual circumstances.

UPDATE ON THE DISAPPEARANCE OF ANNA AND EDWARD GREY

Their parents, Anna and Edward Grey, disappeared in Central Africa while working with a children's medical charity six weeks ago. Since then they have made contact with the twins via a series of Morse code messages sent through the children's watches, but they have asked that Kensington and Maxim tell no one and trust only me. This case note will remain Status Black for all other Pharos agents - including Dame Spencer - until Anna and Edward return or in the event of my death, whereby the information will be automatically disseminated to those with appropriate clearances.

OTHER INFORMATION

Kensington and Maxim continue to run rings around Song, who has been tasked with assisting me to look after the pair. It has been extremely amusing to watch.

CHAPTER 1

⌐⌐⌐⌐⌐ ⌐⌐ ⌐⌐⌐⌐⌐
Target Practice

Kensy ran swiftly, her footsteps soundless on the damp ground. She turned the corner and her heart sank. It was a dead end. She was about to double back when, by chance, she glanced up. There, on the other side of the tightly woven hedge, stood an oak tree perfect for climbing. If she could reach it before he rounded the bend, she'd stand a chance.

Kensy dove onto the ground, her fingernails jamming with dirt as she clawed her way underneath the foliage. With one final push, her legs slithered through. She launched herself

1

at the bottom branch, swinging up and over while trying not to rustle the leaves, then flattened against the trunk and adjusted her night-vision goggles. Her breath created tiny clouds in the darkness.

All was still but for a single silhouette that crept around the corner and down the path. Kensy grinned as she lined him up in the crosshairs. She closed her left eye and squeezed the trigger.

A loud yelp followed by a burst of salty language filled the air.

Kensy stuffed her fist into her mouth to suppress a fit of giggles. Now was not the time to give herself away. She crouched down, straddling the thick bough, and whispered into her headset. "Man down!"

There was a whir and a *thunk* as the pitch-black maze was illuminated by floodlights hidden in the canopies of the surrounding trees. Kensy lifted her arm to shield her eyes and sprang to her feet.

Song's voice came through as clear as crystal from the control room, where he had been monitoring the activity. "Well done, Miss Kensington," he said, the smile in his voice audible. "Your team has emerged triumphant this evening. Please make your way back to the house and we will celebrate with a feast. Mrs. Thornthwaite has been very busy."

"Woo-hoo! Thanks, Song." Kensy did a little victory dance on the tree branch and almost lost her balance. She hoped nobody saw her. "Hey, guys, we did it! Finally!"

There were whoops of joy – some from close by while the rest came over the airwaves.

"Not fair!" Dante moaned. The lad had been sure he'd had the girl cornered. "Kensy's outside the perimeter. Isn't that against the rules?"

"It is not," Kensy argued. "This tree is clearly on the boundary line. There's no need to be such a sore loser, Moretti."

"If Miss Kensington was clever enough to see a vantage point then, I am afraid, Master Dante, that she has done nothing illegal," Song informed the lad, receiving another groan in response.

Kensy leapt from the tree, clearing the hedge and landing hard on the ground inside the maze just as Autumn charged around the corner. Dante had already taken off.

"Go, us!" Autumn exclaimed. She removed her headset and high-fived Kensy.

Even after an hour and a half of intense combat training, the girl was a model of perfection. Autumn's silky black hair remained neatly tied back in a low ponytail with a red ribbon – unlike Kensy's messy locks, which, after scrambling under the hedge, were now sprouting several leaves and a couple of twigs.

The pair were soon joined by Harper and Max, but the rest of their team were still deep inside the labyrinth. Via their earpieces, the children could hear their opponents complaining about how many bruises they were going to have tomorrow.

"Stop your whining, Carlos," Autumn ordered. "At least I had the good grace to shoot you in the bottom. You got me in the head last time, but you didn't hear me going on about it like a big baby."

It was true. Carlos had aimed at the girl's shoulder, but somehow the projectile clipped the edge of Autumn's helmet. The bullets were made of soft rubber and, although the children were fully covered in their sensory slimline body armor, concealed beneath their clothes, the pellets still packed a punch. It was all part of their training – Mr. Nutting and Miss Witherbee, the children's PE and English teachers respectively, were also in charge of weapons instruction and maintained there was a purpose for using rubber bullets instead of something messier but less invasive like paint balls. They reasoned that the children needed regular reminders of the harsh and at times fatal realities of their impending life of service.

Kensy looked at her brother, who possessed an uncanny knack of navigating the maze without running into the usual dead ends. "Can you get us out of here, Max?"

"Sure – follow me," the boy said.

He jogged to the end of the row and turned left, with Kensy, Harper and Autumn in tow. It was a little while before the rest of the group joined them at the entrance. While en route, Max had been called on by a couple of the kids who were horribly lost to offer his guidance. It wasn't too long before everyone was accounted for.

"Congratulations, Kensy." Sachin's dark eyes glinted with good humor. He offered the girl his hand. "Your team was on fire tonight."

There was a murmur of agreement from the rest of the kids. Max hoped his sister wouldn't gloat too much. She had a tendency to do that, which rubbed some people the wrong way and understandably so.

"We couldn't let you beat us three nights in a row," Kensy replied, and checked that she'd flicked the safety catch on her weapon. "It helped that Alfie shot you in the first five minutes."

The burly lad grinned. "I was very proud of that."

Sachin rubbed his shoulder. "You couldn't have taken a step back, maybe? I'm going to have a welt there for weeks."

Alfie shrugged and carried on grinning. "You were right in front of me and you know what Nutters says – he who hesitates is lost."

"Or *she*, but you don't need to hesitate to be lost," Inez said. "If it wasn't for Max's instructions, I'd be camping in the maze tonight. I don't know why I have no sense of direction whatsoever. I really need to work on that."

The others chuckled. It was true – Inez was hopeless. One day during Pharos lessons at school, she'd managed to make her way to Dame Spencer's office at the *Beacon*, several blocks away, when she'd meant to take the secret elevator to the lab.

The group headed back toward the storage shed to put away the equipment.

"Can you believe it's Christmas the day after tomorrow?" Autumn said wistfully. She hooked her arm through Kensy's and gave the girl a squeeze. "I'm forecasting snow."

Kensy cast her eyes upward and frowned. There was a bite to the night air, but there wasn't so much as a hint of frost on the ground. "Really? It doesn't seem cold enough."

"Trust me," Autumn said with a wink.

Kensy rolled her eyes. "Sure – of course there will be snow. I mean, after everything else that's happened in the past month, why wouldn't there be snow at Christmas, right on cue?"

Autumn turned to her friend with a quizzical look.

"It's just that one minute you think you're an ordinary kid with regular parents, whose dad tells the worst jokes and then . . ." Kensy paused, afraid that the trembling in her throat would make its way into her voice.

Autumn pulled the girl into a hug. "We'll find them," she said softly. "Don't ask me how I know it – I've got a good feeling, and my good feelings are usually right."

Kensy nodded and looked across at her brother. The thing was, the twins knew their parents were alive – they just didn't know where they were or why they'd suddenly gone to ground or, worse, if they'd been abducted. When the twins had first traveled to London, they'd received a couple of cryptic messages and then the confirmation, including an instruction to tell no one and to only trust Fitz. Not even Dame Cordelia Spencer – their extraordinary, and until recently top secret grandmother, who also happened to be the head of Pharos – had any idea about the contact. Cordelia had, however, authorized a full-scale operation that involved agents all over the world searching for her son and daughter-in-law. Ed and Anna had been in touch with the twins each week since their first contact, but with no more than a few words to let the kids know they were alive. While Kensy and Max felt guilty keeping this information to themselves, for the moment it simply had to stay that way.

Thankfully, the past month had been so busy they'd had little time to dwell on the situation. On the day they learned the truth about the organization and their grandmother they had been presented with two leather-bound books by Song and Sidney, Cordelia's twin butlers. These had now been studied from cover to cover, revealing much about Pharos and its workings. A spy agency above all others, Pharos had been founded in the ancient lighthouse of the same name in Alexandria, Egypt, by a group of concerned citizens committed to keeping their city safe from crime and evildoing. Over the centuries, its secrets had been passed down through generations until the leadership was bestowed upon their grandfather, Dominic Spencer. His wife, Cordelia, somewhat reluctantly took over as head of the organization following Dominic's untimely death.

Pharos transcended governments, working for the greater good across all countries and cultures. By comparison, the likes of MI6, ASIS and the FBI seemed little more than parochial PR companies, although there was no denying they did some good work on occasion. Pharos had remained under the radar since its inception and it was Dame Spencer's responsibility to see that it stayed that way. She had spent much of her adult life running the *Beacon*, a well-respected tabloid in England. It was a huge business in itself as well as a perfect cover for the agency's clandestine operations. Despite being bombarded with information, Kensy and Max both knew there was still so much to learn.

Carlos looked across and noticed that, even though he was on the winning team tonight, Max hadn't said a word for the past five minutes. Everyone else was chattering excitedly, but he seemed far away. Carlos nudged the lad. "What's up?"

Max offered a weak smile. "It's going to be strange having Christmas without them."

"Well," Carlos said, "if past years are anything to go by, it will still be a celebration you'll never forget – especially if my dad and Mr. MacGregor hit the dance floor again."

Max raised an eyebrow. "What do you mean?"

"You'll see." Carlos grimaced. "Embarrassing doesn't even begin to cover it."

Max grinned. "Sounds like something to look forward to."

CHAPTER 2

ꓕꓵꓣ ꓯꓥꓥꓘꓳꓳ

The jumper

The past few days had been hectic, to say the least. When school had broken up for the two-week Christmas vacation, Kensy and Max, along with the rest of the junior Pharos agents at Central London Free School, had been left in pairs at various train stations around London. They were each handed twenty pounds to find their own way to Dame Spencer's country estate in North Yorkshire. That was something of a challenge given the rail fare was twice that amount.

Since their arrival, the children had

undertaken a variety of intensive training sessions. Unbeknownst to the twins during their first visit, Alexandria was not just Dame Spencer's rural idyll; it was also the countryside headquarters of Pharos, boasting so much more than beautiful gardens and a stunning fountain. The incredibly well-concealed state-of-the-art facilities included an indoor Olympic-sized swimming pool that was housed in what looked from the outside to be a barn, albeit with an entire wall of glass. It featured a hydraulic diving board that could automatically sense the height at which the diver was willing to leap, but was programmed to then rise twenty percent higher. There was also an archery field complete with straw dummies that reacted when hit, the maze where the children would practice their marksmanship, and an enormous blast-proof bunker beneath the stables. Who knew what else they were yet to discover, but one thing was for certain – there were bound to be more surprises in store.

A number of their teachers had accompanied the group on their specialist activities.

Despite being part of Pharos for over a month now, Kensy and Max were still getting their heads around how everything worked. To the outside world, Central London Free School was just a regular school. Eighty percent of the students were ordinary kids, but the remaining twenty percent and every single staff member – from Mrs. Potts in the office, to Mrs. Trimm, the dinner lady; Mr. Reffell, their slightly unhinged history teacher, all the way up to Mr. MacGregor, the headmaster – were Pharos agents and agents-in-training.

The rest of the school staff were due to arrive in time for Christmas, along with the children's families and other agents, whose cover ranged from cab drivers to journalists and many things between. It was to be a huge celebration. According to the program, training would last until midday on Christmas Eve, followed by a party that night. There would be a formal lunch on Christmas Day before guests returned home and some of the children departed for Rome on Mr. Reffell's history tour. It was straight back to school after that. Kensy and Max were looking forward to the trip. At the moment, being busy was a very good thing.

Gordon Nutting and Willow Witherbee intercepted the children as they reached the storage shed – although this wasn't your average farm building. The twins' jaws had almost hit the ground the first time they'd stepped inside. For thirty seconds it appeared exactly as one might expect, with various pieces of gardening equipment neatly organized along the stone walls. Then Miss Witherbee pulled on a hook and the interior transformed into something else entirely. Gun racks flipped out of the walls, hanging rails containing bulletproof body armor rose up from the floor, and various other weapons ranging from handguns to crossbows descended from the ceiling.

"Well done, everyone – except for you, Dante." Gordon Nutting tut-tutted. "How you lasted as long as you did is a complete mystery. You do know, if you stick your head up, it's going to be a target."

Dante grinned. "Must be the luck of the Irish."

"You're Italian, Moretti," Harper quipped. "Which is a good thing because I need a translator on our trip."

"I have an Irish grandmother," the boy replied. "And I will be happy to lend my services as an interpreter, although I haven't decided how much to charge yet."

Harper flicked her blonde ponytail over her shoulder. "I'll buy you a gelato, but that's it."

"Ah, frozen dessert treats." Dante sighed happily. "You do know the way to a young man's language skills."

The teachers and a couple of students remained behind to lock everything away while the rest of the children exited through a door in a high stone wall into the rear garden nearest to the house. Fairy lights twinkled in the trees and hedges though not in the heavens tonight. The patchy afternoon clouds had knitted together like a snug gray blanket, but at least it wasn't quite as cold as it had been.

Max gazed up into the darkness and did a double take. He rubbed his eyes and wondered if he was imagining things. "Hey, look over there," he said, pointing at the sky beyond the roof of the mansion.

"What is it?" Kensy asked, squinting into the distance.

"Someone is up there," Max said, breaking into a run. "They're going to crash!"

"What are you talking about?" Kensy was beginning to think her brother must have taken a hit to the head during the exercise. He was making no sense at all.

But Sachin's eyes had tracked it too. "Oh my gosh. There's a parachute – a roman candle. Whoever it is, is going to hit the ground!"

The children charged after Max, who ran around the side of the house and down the driveway to the field beyond the Atlas fountain. All eyes were glued to the figure in the sky, silently praying for their chute to open.

"Did anyone hear a plane?" Kensy puffed, and was met with a volley of negatives. "Well, how did whoever that is get up there in the first place?"

"Good question," Autumn panted.

"Does anyone from . . . *outside* know about this place?" Kensy couldn't help wondering if there were suddenly going to be hundreds of jumpers raining from the sky, armed with some form of deadly weapon. She was prone to letting her imagination get the better of her.

Max leapt off the ha-ha wall into the field below, sending Dame Spencer's sheep scattering and bleating at the tops of their lungs. Alfie was following close behind but miscued and hooked his foot on a loose stone. He landed flat on his face and half a dozen of the children thudded down on top of him. Fortunately, the hulking lad was a seasoned rugby player and simply shook them off, scrambled to his feet and hurtled over to join Max. The group soon caught up to them and all eyes stared into the sky.

The speed of the parachutist was enthralling, though the likely outcome was absolutely sickening. Yasmina covered her eyes.

"This is going to be messy," Dante murmured, unable to look away.

Moments before impact, a chute opened. It was a giant of a thing, at least three times bigger than usual, which stopped the jumper in their tracks with a sharp jolt. The children watched as the figure floated to the ground like a feather and landed deftly on their feet. At that second, the clouds parted to reveal a full moon, the light glinting off the jumper's silver suit. The interloper removed their helmet and goggles and realized that they had drawn quite a different audience to the flock of sheep they'd been expecting.

"Good grief, what are you lot doing here?" the man said. "I rather fancied a surprise arrival, but my stealth clearly leaves a lot to be desired."

At the sound of the man's voice, Carlos broke into a grin. "Agent Spencer, is that you?"

"At your service. Whoever's asking?" the man replied.

"It's Rodriguez, sir," the boy said, stepping forward.

Kensy and Max looked at one another and then at the man, their eyes wide. They'd never even met their dad's brother before and now here he was. Rupert Spencer was clearly a man of action and intrigue given his choice of transport.

"Oh, hello, Carlos. I hope you're up for a spin around the track. If I recall, I still owe you a walloping after you cheated last year," Rupert said. He fiddled with the sleeve of his suit and, in the blink of an eye, the voluminous silk parachute shot toward him while simultaneously folding itself neatly into the pack he was wearing.

Carlos folded his arms across his chest. "Except that I *didn't* cheat."

Max nudged his sister. "Rupert?" he mouthed.

"Where did you come from?" Alfie asked. "We didn't hear a plane."

Agent Spencer betrayed a hint of a smile. "Good – that was the plan," he replied and, with his helmet tucked under one arm, he leapt onto the ha-ha wall and strode off toward the house.

While the others descended into a raft of speculation, Kensy and Max were at a complete loss. *That* was their Uncle Rupert?

"Do you think he saw us?" Kensy asked as they made their way back to the house.

"It's hard to tell," Max replied, deep in thought. Perhaps their uncle hadn't realized they were there. Max wanted to give him the benefit of the doubt, because if Rupert was aware, it seemed pretty clear that he didn't care to know them at all.

CHAPTER 3

ⴹⵓⵍ⟨◇ ◻ⴹⵊⵡⴹⴹⵕ

UNCK RUPORT

Cordelia Spencer looked up from the open newspaper on her desk. She'd been marveling at the ingenuity of a real estate advertisement that had been placed by one of her agents. They were trialing a new form of photographic coding and it seemed to be working brilliantly. A movement out of the corner of her eye caught her attention. She glanced over at the wall of screens and was surprised to see her younger son charge through the front door. She hadn't been expecting him – at least not this evening – and, considering he'd been off-grid for the past month or so, she was keen to find out exactly what he'd been working on. By the looks of his face, it was probably his tan more than anything. Sometimes she wondered at the wisdom of having promoted him to Agent X status. He was still prodding her to take over Ed's Y ranking, but that wasn't going to happen anytime soon.

She'd sent Rupert several messages about the twins, receiving a single-word response: Brilliant. Given she'd also told him that his brother and sister-in-law were missing and there were few leads at this stage, despite having deployed a huge number of resources to try to track them down, it seemed a rather odd and unsatisfying reply. But that was Rupert. Of her two children, he had always been the more difficult to read.

Cordelia opened the top drawer of her mahogany desk and pulled out two velvet jewelry cases – one long and slim, the other smaller and rectangular. They contained Maxim and Kensington's Christmas gifts. She had all but resigned herself that this day would never come – although it was bittersweet. If only Anna and Ed had been found. She knew full well that the chances of them being really dead this time were higher than ever, especially the longer they were gone.

There was a rap on the door. Cordelia's two West Highland terriers, Wellington and Mackintosh, looked up from the rug in front of the fire and thumped their tails.

"Come in," Cordelia called, returning the boxes to the drawer.

Fitz strode into the room and shut the door behind him. "I thought I'd find you hiding here. The place is a bit of a madhouse. I see the dogs have got the right idea – keeping out of everyone's way."

Cordelia smiled at her nephew. Having him back after all these years was wonderful. From the time he was a toddler, Fitz had been one of her favorite people in the world. "Did you know Rupert has arrived?" she asked.

Fitz looked at her in surprise. "No, he's one person I haven't bumped into," he said, sinking into the chair opposite Cordelia. "Do you have any idea where he's been?"

"I imagine I'll find out soon enough," she replied, absently fiddling with the rings on her left hand.

"I'm afraid I need to head off first thing in the morning," Fitz said firmly.

Cordelia frowned. "But what about the children? It's Christmas Eve tomorrow. They'll be so disappointed. They're going to find it hard enough, let alone with you gone too."

Fitz rubbed his head. Ever since he came to terms with the fact he was going bald, he'd found the feel of it rather soothing. "They'll understand."

"I doubt it." Cordelia stood up and smoothed her navy skirt, then strode over to the table beneath the window. She poured herself a whisky from the crystal decanter. "Unless the three of you know something you're not telling me."

She offered Fitz a drink, which he politely declined.

"I've got a lead," he said, choosing not to add more. Over the past six weeks, he had found it difficult watching the woman suffer, and he would hate to toy with her hopes. Cordelia was, in a way, more like a second mother to him than an aunt. "I'll speak with Kensy and Max tonight."

He desperately wanted to tell her, but Anna and Ed had been very specific. If there was a mole inside Pharos, any hint that they were alive would jeopardize everything – and not only their safety, but the children's too. It wasn't how he preferred to play things, but that was the current state of affairs. He was also tired of fending off the twins' questions about why he and their parents had faked their deaths in the first place. It hadn't taken them long to work out that "we wanted a normal life" was little more than a flimsy excuse, particularly as their lives traversing the globe and living in a different ski resort each season were pretty far removed from most children's experiences. Unfortunately, the ill-fated mission that preceded the three of them disappearing from the face of the earth was still classified Status Red, meaning that only Cordelia and a handful of agents knew exactly what had happened.

Even Fitz's own mother was in the dark – a fact that had eaten away at him for the past eleven years.

Cordelia tucked a stray strand of hair behind her left ear. "You know your mother is going to be disappointed too. It's been years since Mim's had you home for the holidays. I'm sure she thought you'd never be back again . . . I suppose we all make our sacrifices for the greater good, don't we?" She smiled sadly, wondering when exactly she had begun to sound so bitter.

Fitz shifted in his seat. There it was again – a glimmer of the pain Cordelia had been trying so hard to hide. "Mim's fine. She already knows and she's promised to focus all her energy on the children for me." He stood up and walked over to his aunt. "I just wanted to say goodbye. I'll be gone before dawn and there will be so many people here that you won't even miss me."

Cordelia arched an eyebrow and took a sip of her drink. "Don't remind me. Mrs. Thornthwaite is positively apoplectic down in the kitchen – I wanted to stop by and see how my puddings had turned out, but I don't dare for fear of being roped into hours of turkey-stuffing."

"I'll be back as soon as I can," Fitz said, laughing.

"Thank you, darling." Cordelia put down her glass and clasped her nephew's hands. "You've done a brilliant job with those children – they're even more magnificent than I could ever have imagined."

Fitz flushed. It didn't matter how old he was; every word of praise from Cordelia transported him back to his ten-year-old self seeking her approval. "I certainly didn't raise them on my own. Anna and Ed are wonderful parents, Cordelia. If only we can get them back here in one piece, you could see so for yourself."

Cordelia's eyes glistened as Fitz kissed her cheek. Then he turned and walked from the room. For several minutes after he'd left, she stood there staring into the firelight. She'd gone over things in her mind more times than she cared to remember. Ed and Anna were far too clever to have been caught in a rebel uprising. Anyway, recent intelligence suggested there was no evidence of them having been in Africa at all. The more she thought about it, the more it made sense – there was only one reason they would have broken their cover and left the children.

Cordelia crossed her hands over her pounding heart. If anyone could find them, it would be Fitz, and if he knew more than he was prepared to admit, then she needed to butt out and let him get on with it.

* * *

As the children burst through the front doors, there was much chatter and conjecture about Rupert's arrival. Song was pleased to see them, having wondered where on earth they'd all disappeared to. Their supper was waiting for them in the conservatory.

"Why would he do it?" Inez mused. She tightened the band that was holding back her copper curls. "I mean, it's not ideal to skydive in cloudy weather – unless he was testing some top secret new technology."

The children agreed that seemed the most rational scenario and were keen to find out what sort of aircraft had provided such stealth-like means. They followed their noses and charged down the hall toward the conservatory while Kensy and Max hung back.

"Song, do you know where our uncle is?" Max asked.

"I suspect he has gone upstairs to change," the man replied. Song was momentarily distracted by a patch of dust on a side table and made a mental note to do another round with the feather duster when everyone had retired for the evening.

"He didn't even have a bag with him," Max said.

"Your uncle still has a bedroom upstairs – just down the hall from you two," Song said. "His wardrobe is fully stocked so it does not matter if he arrives without so much as a pair of underpants. I hope he likes the superhero ones I ordered the other day."

The twins laughed.

"He didn't even say hello," Kensy said. She looked at Song from beneath knitted eyebrows. "Are you sure he knows we even exist? Or cares?"

The butler nodded. "I am certain of it, but don't expect too much of him. He can be . . ." The man grasped for the right words. "Confucius says that only the wisest and stupidest men never change."

"And which category would you place me in, old man?" a voice said from behind them.

Song and the twins spun around to see Rupert standing on the staircase. How long he'd been there was anyone's guess. Kensy couldn't help but giggle nervously.

"Good evening, sir," Song said, without missing a beat. He bowed – but not as deeply as he usually would, Max noted. "It is good to see you again. I hear that you made quite the entrance."

Rupert sauntered down the stairs, smiling at them. He was now casually dressed in a pair of jeans with a light-pink shirt and a gray sweater slung around his shoulders. "In answer to your question, my dear Kensington, yes, I am very much aware of you and your brother. In fact, I have been *dying* to meet you both ever since I found out you were here. I've been away on assignment – these things do have a tendency to get in the way of even the best-laid plans. I suppose you'll understand that soon enough."

He considered the children carefully.

"Your parents must be so proud," he continued, and Kensy was moved to see his eyes begin to water. She was starting to feel quite guilty for accusing her uncle of being disinterested. "Sorry, it's just that you're both so much like Eddie." Rupert pulled a handkerchief from his pocket and dabbed at his eyes.

Max hesitated for a moment before pushing his shoulders back and walking toward the man with his hand outstretched. Rupert shook it, then wrapped his muscular arms around the boy. "It's good to meet you, Uncle Rupert," Max said, realizing immediately that there was something uncomfortable about the man's embrace. Max didn't know what it was – perhaps it felt forced.

"Uncle Rupert," the man repeated. "I like the sound of that." He looked at Kensy and grinned. "Do you have a hug for your favorite uncle too?"

Kensy smiled and embraced him. She'd been thinking about the uncanny similarities between Rupert and their father – and Max too. "You look a lot like Dad," she said, stepping back.

"Oh, no. I'm far more handsome than Ed," the man scoffed. He laughed and added, "Only because I'm younger and have much better dress sense."

Song pressed his lips together to avoid the risk of opening his mouth.

Encouraged by her uncle's candor, Kensy decided that now was as good a time as any to put him on the spot. "Do you know what really happened to Mum and Dad and why they left Pharos in the first place?" she asked. "Fitz says that they all wanted a normal life, but we think there's more to it – our lives were hardly normal."

Max glared at his sister, wishing she'd waited until they knew the man a little better before giving him the third degree.

Song cleared his throat. "Miss Kensington, perhaps you should allow your uncle to tell you all that he knows in due time."

Rupert smirked. "There's nothing to tell, really. I don't know any more than you do. Your mother was pregnant – she had cold feet about bringing up her children inside Pharos, so they staged their own deaths and we all went along with it – except that for quite a long time I was led to believe they were dead, the same as everybody else. Bit of a shock to discover that I'd been hoodwinked. Old Confucius here would know the real story – he outranked me for years until recently, but Mummy's probably sworn him to secrecy. It's like that around here."

Song shifted from one foot to the other, causing the floorboards to groan.

Rupert raised his eyebrows at the butler. "Isn't there somewhere you should be? Tables to wait? Drinks to pour? The children and I have a lot of catching up to do. We'll be in the library – rustle us up something to eat and I'd like a glass of '86 Grange. I'm quite partial to an Australian drop – must be because Mummy came from convict stock, although I suppose we can forgive her that."

Song puffed out his chest. "Master Maxim and Miss Kensington are having supper in the conservatory with their classmates. Afterward, they are required to attend a debriefing led by Mr. Nutting and Miss Witherbee on this evening's training exercise."

Rupert cocked his head to one side. "I didn't realize Willow was here. I'll pop by and say hello. She won't mind if I commandeer the children. After all, they are my long-lost niece and nephew."

Max bit down on his thumbnail. "Um, Uncle Rupert, if you don't mind, I think we should go," he said, sounding less certain than he felt. He didn't want the other kids to think he and Kensy got any special treatment. "Kensy and I are so new at this spy business that we really need to learn everything we can."

Kensy rolled her eyes. Trust Max to spoil the fun. The last thing she felt like doing after dinner was going over Nutter's and Busybee's boring notes on a scenario her team had won. Although the fact that she had bragging rights appealed to her, so there was that at least.

"Well, I can see which of you is the *fun* twin." Rupert gave Kensy a wink.

The girl giggled then, remembering herself, chastened. "Max is probably right," she said grudgingly. "Especially after what happened in London."

Max caught his sister's eye and touched his left ear. It was so quick and natural that no one would have guessed it was their special signal. Thankfully, Kensy noticed and closed her mouth. He didn't want her discussing all that with Uncle Rupert. It just didn't seem like the right time to regale him with the story of how they had evaded being kidnapped – twice – when they still had no idea who had been after them. Kensy was positive it was one of the gardeners from Alexandria called

Shugs, but Max and Fitz didn't share her conviction.

Rupert shrugged. "Suit yourself, but I can't guarantee I'll be here later on. I'm sure there's a party somewhere with my name on it."

"We'll do our best to get away early," Kensy promised. She desperately wanted to spend some time with her uncle. He reminded her so much of their father and she had a hunch that he would tell them things no one else would. Besides, he was clearly very adventurous and didn't take himself too seriously – no doubt he could teach them loads of things too.

But Max wasn't so eager. For someone who had just shed a tear for them a few minutes ago, their Uncle Rupert seemed almost disinterested now. Fitz had mentioned on more than a couple of occasions how difficult the man was to pin down, and right at the moment Max thought that was a pretty fair assessment.

CHAPTER 4

JOUƎՐOC
Debrief

Ida Thornthwaite pushed up her sleeves and scooped a large helping of lasagna onto Kensy's plate. "Well done, dear," the woman said. "I heard you outsmarted the enemy tonight."

Kensy nodded, beaming. That meant a lot coming from the single most deadly knife thrower in the agency. "It was about time, really. I was beginning to think I had no strategic skills at all."

"I'm sure that's not true. If you're anything like your father, you'll have tactical activities mastered in no time," Mrs. Thornthwaite said with a wink. She turned to smile at Max, who requested a serving of spaghetti Bolognese and some garlic bread.

"This looks amazing," the boy said, heaping a mountain of grated Parmesan on top. He was ravenous. The children were meant to have had a snack before training, but Max had lost track of time in the library, studying a new book he'd found on codes.

Kensy wrinkled her nose at him. "Are you sure you wouldn't like some pasta with all that cheese?"

"Ha ha," her brother replied, but when Mrs. Thornthwaite held up her spoon to offer more, he happily passed her his plate. Max inhaled deeply. "If this tastes half as good as it smells, I'll be in heaven."

"I couldn't help myself tonight," Ida said, pleased that her efforts were appreciated. "After hearing you lot talk of Italy and your upcoming trip, I thought it was only fitting. I haven't been there since we brought down a scurrilous prime minister over twenty years ago, but I just adore the food."

The twins grinned. The woman looked around and leaned forward. "Dame Spencer won't be happy to see the grocery bill. The price of imported Italian pasta is through the roof at the moment. I couldn't believe my eyes!"

It seemed strange to think that the elderly cook had once been an active agent. Up until a couple of days ago, when the woman had given the most enthralling lesson on handling all manner of blades, Kensy had only ever thought of her as a grandmotherly figure. Round and squishy, Ida Thornthwaite possessed a smile as warm and comforting as the winter meals she prepared. Kensy now knew better. Mrs. Thornthwaite's skills were lethal.

The twins thanked the woman again and joined their friends, although they had very little time to eat as Miss Witherbee was barking orders to hurry up. The woman reminded Kensy of a greyhound – skinny and angular – but with the temperament of a cranky terrier.

Kensy and Max scoffed down their meals and scampered over to join the tail end of the line of children being ushered from the conservatory via a concealed doorway, which for all the world looked like a wall of mirrors. They headed down a set of stone steps to a passageway beneath the rear courtyard and into their classroom in the bunker under the stables.

As to be expected, this was no ordinary teaching space. For a start, there was a complete absence of desks and chairs. Instead, the room was arranged in the style of an amphitheater. The children's names were lit up on the riser where they were required to sit and, to date, their seating arrangements had changed each time so that they never sat next to the same person twice. On the opposite curved wall was a huge screen that the teachers had used several times now during lessons. Willow Witherbee was sitting in a single chair close to the door.

Mr. Nutting, resplendent in his customary navy-and-red tracksuit, stood in front of them. A three-dimensional plan of the maze appeared between him and the children, floating three feet from the ground. Max had worked out it was a hologram that was somehow projected from below, but he was yet to understand the finer details.

The teacher scratched at the side of his nose and zipped up his jacket. Kensy noticed that, for a man whose face was still youthful, he had more than his fair share of gray hairs. It was probably stressful being a teacher and even more so working undercover as an agent.

"Shall we take a look at how things played out tonight?" Mr. Nutting began. "As always, I want you to think strategy and where you went wrong."

Avatars of each one of the children appeared inside the hologram of the maze. The students leaned forward in their seats, eager to get through the activity as quickly as possible. It had been Harper's birthday yesterday and the girl had leftover treats that she'd promised to share once they were in their dorms.

"Can you see your mistake, Sachin?" Mr. Nutting pointed at the avatar of Alfie with a long wand-like implement that shot a glowing beam from its tip.

Sachin grimaced as he watched Alfie take him out at almost point-blank range within the first minute. "I was too busy looking for Max, sir. I wasn't paying attention to anything behind me," he replied. "And I might have been thinking about who was going to be our opening batsman in the upcoming Melbourne Boxing Day match."

There was a titter of giggles from the other children as Gordon Nutting shook his head. "Well, in this business you need laser focus and eyes in the back of your head. There is no time to be daydreaming about cricket."

"Yes, sir," Sachin said meekly.

The man was about to continue when he caught sight of Inez and Yasmina whispering in the back. Gordon pointed his wand toward them, a red dot centering on Inez's forehead bang on one of her freckles. It took a few moments for the girls to realize that everyone was staring at them.

"What?" Yasmina said, before spotting the glaring sign on her friend's brow. She pressed her forefinger to her lips and swallowed.

Inez looked around. "Do I have something in my teeth?" she asked.

Carlos shook his head. "I don't think so, but Mr. Nutting might be about to kill you with his laser pointer."

The children laughed and Inez shrunk down in her seat.

"You're lucky I'm not in the mood for blood tonight, girls." Mr. Nutting sighed. "Now, could we please get back to the task at hand?"

The footage continued and there were several times the teacher sped up the action. Kensy tapped her foot, wishing he would play the whole thing on fast-forward. She really wanted to get back inside and find her uncle before he went out. Miss Witherbee also seemed eager to be on her way. She had stood up from her seat and positioned herself by the door.

"Let's run through the last five minutes to see what led to the ultimate demise of Sachin's team," Mr. Nutting said. "Actually, perhaps you would like to take the children through this section, Miss Witherbee."

All eyes turned to the woman, who was glued to her phone. She was smiling to herself and seemed far, far away.

"Earth to Willow," the man said, not bothering to hide his exasperation.

The ripple of laughter from the children roused the woman.

"Sorry," she said, her cheeks flushing. She dropped her phone into her pocket and straightened. "What did you say, Mr. Nutting?"

"Forget it," the man muttered, and proceeded to walk the room through the final part of the exercise before firing questions at the children about what they could and should have done differently. He praised Kensy's quick thinking and flexibility to get herself to the tree and then invited the group to offer some alternative scenarios.

Carlos was the first to volunteer. He had been watching the playback carefully and had devised a plan where he could have covered Dante if only they'd thought to work together. He moved the figures around in the maze with a swipe of his hand and, seconds later, the outcome was completely different, with Kensy being the one who was shot. She also fell out of the tree, which garnered guffaws of laughter.

Kensy rolled her eyes and resisted the urge to rub her shoulder. "Gee, thanks, Carlos. That would have hurt."

Mr. Nutting asked for another version of events and this time it was Max who put up his hand. Kensy eyeballed her brother, trying to send him a telepathic message to make it quick, but it seemed that he had reimagined the entire evening and come up with several ways their team could have finished off the others in half the time it had actually taken. To his credit, his ideas were pretty amazing. Even Mr. Nutting was impressed.

It was just after nine o'clock when the children were dismissed and, although they were bone tired, the twins set off in search of their uncle. Kensy shivered as they wandered the halls, having left her coat back in the classroom. But the man was nowhere to be found. It was probably for the best given the twins could barely keep their eyes open. When Mim said she'd seen headlights on the driveway, they gave up the search.

The twins made their way down a long corridor toward the back door. At least six feet wide, the passage housed a range of ornate antique furniture, including bureaus and sideboards, a grandmother and grandfather clock and a rather startling brown bear standing on its hind legs and baring its very pointy incisors. Song told them his name was Frank and he'd been a pet many years ago, when it was a fanciful trend in Victorian England to keep exotic animals. Apparently, the creature had romped about the gardens like a faithful hound and was known for his placid temperament. But Kensy and Max's great-grandfather had decided that, in death, Frank might prefer to be a little fierce – hence the stance and sharpened teeth.

"What did you think of Uncle Rupert?" Kensy asked.

Max shrugged. "I think I should reserve my judgement until we've spent some more time together."

"He was only kidding around – what he said about me being the fun twin," Kensy said, giving Max a jovial elbow to the ribs.

"He doesn't even know us," Max said indignantly. "And I can be as much fun as you when I want to be."

Outside, an eerie mist had settled over the courtyard.

"Do you think anyone would notice if we slept in the house tonight?" Kensy said. She wasn't keen to trek back to the stables in the gloomy weather. The thought of her queen-sized bed and feather-down quilt – not to mention that enormous claw-foot bathtub – was far more tempting than the narrow bunk allotted to each agent-in-training, the shared bathroom and incessant snoring. Then again, there had been the promise of Harper's leftover birthday treats.

Max didn't have time to answer as Song appeared from behind a potted palm, where he had just reclaimed Wellie and Mac's latest bone stash.

"Good evening, Miss Kensington, Master Maxim," the butler greeted them, a huge bone dangling from his left hand. "I would strongly suggest that you return to your colleagues this evening. You are on an official training camp and it would not do your service history any favors to skip out, especially on the last night." His face softened and he pushed his glasses back from the tip of his nose. "Besides, I thought you were enjoying the company of your peers."

"We are," Max said, and looked at Kensy. "At least, I am."

Kensy nodded. "I am too. It's just miserable out there and I left my coat in the classroom."

"I can show you another way," Song said with a twinkle in his eye. "It is much warmer."

The twins were suddenly wide-awake.

"Is it a secret tunnel?" Kensy asked. The girl was certain Alexandria had only given up a fraction of its secrets to date. Every day there were new discoveries to be made — extra rooms, endless passageways and subterranean lairs.

"It is my *favorite* secret tunnel," Song said.

Although Kensy and Max now had their own beautiful bedrooms on the first floor of the house, for the duration of the training camp they were bunking in with everyone else in the stables. Located to the left-hand rear of the mansion, the magnificent Victorian structure had once housed an exquisite collection of steeds but had been converted into accommodation many years ago now. It provided sleeping quarters for the entire Pharos student body and at least six of their teachers, who stayed in the private suites at either end of the long corridors. While the estate still retained working stables and an equestrian center, they were situated on the other side of the village.

The girls' dormitory was at one end of the building and the boys' was at the other, separated by a large sitting room in the middle with comfy couches, a cinema, pool and table tennis tables, a sumo boxing ring complete with suits that had the children hysterical with laughter anytime it was used, an electronic dartboard as well as an array of board games and books. It reminded Kensy of the game room in the cellar where Song had entertained them for hours during their first visit – except there was no bowling alley here. There was, however, a zip line, which launched from the gallery above and sent the children pummeling toward a pit of foam bricks at the other end.

Rows of bunk beds lined the walls of the dorm rooms, with large bathrooms in the corners containing six showers and toilets. They also had a pulley system, which former students had rigged up years ago, allowing them to trade midnight snacks, not only in their own dorms but between rooms as well. These days they used a drone, which was far more efficient as long as someone remembered to open the doors. Kensy was sleeping on the top bunk right by the entrance with Autumn below. Yasmina and Harper were beside them.

Song led the children through to the back of the kitchen and yet more rooms they'd never seen before – there were larders and pantries and a huge door that looked like the access to a bank vault.

Kensy's eyes lit up. "Is this where Granny keeps her real treasures as opposed to all the junk upstairs?"

Song frowned and arched his left eyebrow. He turned the small device in the center of the door this way and that, listening for the clicks, then spun the giant wheel. Kensy and Max peered into the darkness. The butler flicked a switch and beckoned for the children to follow him. Then he stopped and the twins realized that the floor beneath them had started moving.

"Whoa." Kensy grabbed hold of her brother in an effort to steady herself. They were on something akin to a moving walkway, like you might find at an airport.

Max laughed with incredulity when he saw what else the passage contained. Concealed lighting illuminated an array of artworks. "It's a gallery!" the lad exclaimed.

"These are the most valuable works in Dame Spencer's collection," Song replied with a nod.

Kensy peered at a three-dimensional study

in colored pasta. "That's my name on there," she said, having no recollection at all of making it. They glided toward the next masterpiece.

"I remember painting that in second grade in Banff." Max shook his head. "Thank goodness we're going to be spies because, if Granny ever thought we were potential artists, she must be sorely disappointed."

The children marveled at the display and noticed that there were plenty of their father's and uncle's endeavors too. Rupert's were actually quite good – particularly a self-portrait Song told them he'd created for his A levels.

"It's lovely that Granny thinks these are worthy of being framed," Kensy said. "Most parents throw them out after they've been on the fridge for six months."

Song clasped his hands behind his back and nodded. "Your grandmother has kept everything."

"I don't know if that's cute or creepy," Max said with a smile.

A set of six intermittently spaced spiral staircases appeared in the distance.

"Now, I just need to remember which is which," Song said. He tapped his fingers on his forehead for a second then clapped his hands, bringing the walkway to a standstill. "This is your exit, Master Maxim," he said, pointing to the second set of stairs. "It will take you up to your dorm room. Once you are inside, it will be impossible to release the hatch from above, so do not get any ideas about exploring with your friends after lights-out."

Max said good night and scurried away. As he stepped on the fourth tread from the top, a panel opened above his head. The boy emerged from the middle of the floor and narrowly missed being clobbered by a football Alfie had kicked across the room. The boys were stunned to see him. Just like Song said, as soon as Max was through, the hatch closed and was completely invisible to the naked eye.

"Okay, so which one's mine?" Kensy said.

Song scratched his head. He always got this wrong, although he wasn't about to admit that now. It was bad enough that, one night many years ago, he had accidentally directed a young agent-in-training into the headmaster's quarters. The man was in the middle of his evening yoga session, mid headstand, when the hatch lifted and catapulted him against the wall. The headmaster had leapt to his feet and thwacked the unsuspecting girl with a karate kick to the torso before he realized his mistake. "There," Song said, pointing to the second staircase from the end, and clapped his hands to start moving again.

As they drew close, Kensy leapt off and rushed to the top, hoping the girls hadn't eaten all of Harper's treats already. She scrambled up and out, ready to be the center of attention. As the trapdoor closed, however, it dawned on Kensy that this wasn't her dorm room at all. She took in the smaller space with its canopied double bed and rolltop desk. The decor was more in keeping with the main house and there were several lamps and a cozy-looking armchair in the corner too.

"I don't know why you couldn't have waited for me," a woman whined over the sound of running water. "I would have loved to escape for the night."

Kensy recognized the voice and gasped. She raced toward the door, wincing at the sound of the floorboards creaking beneath her feet. The bathroom tap stopped and she heard the doorknob turning. Panicking, Kensy dove under the four-poster bed and held her breath.

Willow Witherbee walked out of the bathroom and looked around. Kensy could see her feet and the hem of her dressing gown coming closer and closer until she could have reached out and touched the woman's painted toes.

"Sorry, I thought I heard something," Willow said. "Honestly, if any of those kids come banging at my door in the middle of the night, I am going to pretend to be dead." She paused. "It's okay. Shugs is on it. First thing."

At the mention of that name, a shiver ran down Kensy's spine. Despite Fitz assuring her that it couldn't have been Shugs who had abducted her and Max in London, she was convinced he was wrong. She just had to find a way to prove it.

Annoyingly, Kensy was stuck under the bed for almost an hour. Willow Witherbee was in and out of the bathroom another four times before she finally hopped under the covers – except, not a minute later, she sighed and was up again. When the symphonic explosions rang out from the bathroom, Kensy was seized by an equally violent fit of giggles she was sure would blow her cover. The girl clamped her hands over her mouth and tried to think Zen thoughts. If there was any accompanying smell, she was done for.

"Oh dear," Willow said out loud as she climbed back into the bedroom. "No baked beans for you tomorrow morning, young lady."

With commendable effort, Kensy managed to regain her composure and waited an eternity until the woman finally switched off the lamp and began to snore. She then slid out from her hiding spot, crawled across the floor and turned the door handle, only daring to breathe once she was safely on the other side.

CHAPTER 5

DOWN AMON THE DEAD MEN

For the third morning in a row, Kensy was awake well before dawn. She surveyed the room, where everyone else was still fast asleep. Harper let out a little grunt and rolled over, but within seconds her breathing was deep and even. Kensy peered over the edge of the bunk at Autumn. She didn't want to wake the girl, but she needed to go for a run to clear her head. She had dreamt about her parents last night and, while she couldn't remember the details, it had left her feeling as if a cage full of guinea pigs was gnawing away at her stomach lining.

Kensy slipped silently from the top bunk, grabbed her tracksuit and sneakers and tiptoed into the bathroom. She scribbled a note and placed it on her pillow in case anyone woke up and wondered where she'd gone. The girl then tiptoed to the door, opening and closing it with the gentlest of clicks. She was feeling quite proud of herself when a clock chimed, sending her skyward. As if it wasn't bad enough having a zillion noisy timepieces inside the house, there was a huge grandfather clock in the hallway of the stables too. It had just gone six. Kensy reached the main door and was surprised to see her brother emerge via the sitting room. He was also dressed and had a flashlight in his hand.

"What are you doing?" he whispered. Kensy wasn't usually up at this hour.

"Going for a run," she whispered back. "I couldn't sleep."

"Me too," he said. "Fancy some company?"

Kensy nodded. She was glad of the chance to talk with him, away from everyone else.

The twins exited through the main stable door, the cold winter air chilling their noses and cheeks as they made their way toward the walled garden and around to the back of the building. The moon cast an eerie glow.

"Where do you want to go?" Max asked.

"Anywhere," Kensy said, breaking into a jog.

The pair soon fell into a rhythm, their footsteps crunching on the gravel path. They ran past the maze and through an open field toward the jagged cliffs. There was a path that hugged the coastline. A way off in the distance, perched on the most easterly point, was a lighthouse. Every fifteen seconds, a beam of light illuminated the inky sea.

"Do you want to run out there?" Kensy suggested, barely panting.

"Better not," Max said. "It's a long way, and we have to be back in time for breakfast. Let's look at that place instead." He aimed his flashlight across the field, the beam connecting with a building he'd noticed yesterday when they were training.

They diverted off the trail and ran side by side in silence, their pace quickening.

Somewhere in the distance they could hear the clattering of an engine and saw the flickering of headlights, but were too far away to get a proper look at the vehicle. Seconds later, it was gone.

"Do you sometimes feel like we went to sleep on our last night in Australia and we still haven't woken up yet and all of this is some kind of crazy dream?" Kensy said.

"Every day," Max replied. "But then I remember it's real and this is our life and we'd better get used to it. Even if . . ." He paused and swallowed his words. "Even *when* Mum and Dad come back, I can't imagine we'll just up and leave. Can you?"

Kensy stopped, her chest heaving. She shook her head, struggling to catch her breath. "I don't want to."

Max halted a few paces ahead and turned to face her. He was surprised to see his sister was close to tears.

"We've only just met Granny and Mim and Song and everyone else. I don't want to lose them," she said.

"Me neither." Max shook his head. "And we don't really know Uncle Rupert at all. He intrigues me."

Kensy grinned, brushing at her eyes with the back of her hand. "Intrigues or annoys?"

"Not sure yet," Max said. "Come on, I'll race you to the wall over there."

"Okay, but prepare to lose, little brother." Kensy began to count down from five but sprinted on two.

"Hey!" Max shouted, and sped after her.

The twins galloped across the field, reaching the wall that encircled the building at almost exactly the same time.

"You cheated," Max panted, his breaths punctuating the still air.

Kensy scoffed. "I just gave myself a head start, that's all."

Even in the predawn light, the children could see that it was an impressive structure with a domed roof and Doric columns. They jogged around the wall until they found a set of steps.

"What do you think it is?" Kensy asked, bounding up two flights.

"Maybe it's a chapel or something," Max said, ever the pragmatist.

"Or the world's fanciest garden shed, more like. Hey, there's a door!" Kensy raced toward it. Finding it locked, Kensy reached up and pulled out her new hair clip. She'd forgotten to wear it yesterday and had been in big trouble with Mrs. Vanden Boom.

Max wandered around the terrace, trying to find another way in, but seconds later, Kensy pushed the door open.

"Are you coming or not?" she called.

Max ran back to join his sister. "That was quick, even for you."

"It helps when you have the Swiss Army knife of hair clips," she replied, returning it to the maelstrom of her unruly locks.

Max's eyebrows jumped up. He was still getting used to the amazing gadgets available to them since joining Pharos and thought the girls' hair clips, with their array of tools and weapons, were spectacular. He almost wished he could wear one too.

They walked inside and Max moved his

flashlight about. There were carved niches in the walls with polished brass plaques above.

Kensy frowned. "What is this place?"

"I believe it's a guesthouse of sorts," Max replied, smiling to himself.

"But there's nothing in here – where are the beds?" Kensy took the flashlight and pointed it at one of the inscriptions. Their grandfather's name was written on it and there was a short spiel about him underneath.

Kensy's eyes widened when she realized that this was the type of guesthouse where everyone was staying permanently. "Um, I think we're in the family crypt."

"Uh-huh."

"But where are they?" Kensy whispered, as if she might wake someone up.

"I'd say they're down below – or in the walls. There was another floor, remember? We had to come up two flights of steps to get here."

Kensy shuddered. "Eww, gross. Let's go."

"Throw me the flashlight," Max said.

Kensy tossed it as she reached the door.

Max read several more plaques before something on the floor caught his attention. In the center of the marble surface was a perfect circle and within it were the numbers zero to one hundred and forty-four. It was gibberish to most people, but not to Max. He mumbled the numbers and some variations then stepped on them in an order that seemed to make sense. First zero then one, one again, two, three, five, eight, thirteen, twenty-one, thirty-four, fifty-five, eighty-nine and, finally, one hundred and forty-four.

"Come on, Max," Kensy hissed from the doorway. "This place gives me the creeps. It's full of dea–"

There was a loud grating sound as the marble slab slid away to reveal a spiral staircase rising up from the floor. Without a backward glance, Max disappeared. Kensy was at a loss for words. This wasn't like her brother at all. He was always the careful one – she practically had to drag him along on any adventure. Not to be outdone, Kensy scampered after him. "If we come across one skeleton, I will never forgive you," she called, her threat bouncing around the walls.

Max was just about to step off the last tread when he halted and hung back. Kensy crashed into him, sending her brother flying forward. He gripped the banister and spun around, pulling himself back onto the step before his feet could touch the ground below.

"Why did you stop?" Kensy demanded.

"Because I think I might have ended up like that guy." Max exhaled and shone the flashlight onto the marble floor. There, in front of them, was a mouse that had been sliced right through the middle.

Kensy gasped. "Oh."

Max fished around in his hoodie pocket and pulled out a chocolate bar he'd squirreled away the day before. He threw it onto the floor and waited, but nothing happened. Maybe he was wrong. He leaned forward just as a checker-board of razor-sharp guillotines thrust upward, cutting the chocolate bar clean in half.

"Whoa," Kensy breathed. "That could have

been us. Whatever's down here must be important."

Max could feel his heart thumping in his chest.

"There's got to be a way to turn it off," Kensy reasoned.

Max felt under the metal railing of the banister and bobbed down to take a closer look. There was a small switch. He pushed it and the steel blades retracted.

"Are you sure it's safe?" Kensy asked.

"There's only one way to find out." Max leapt off the last step and into the circular room.

It was much bigger than the floor upstairs. A bench ran all the way around and above, and below it were literally hundreds of drawers, each bearing a number.

Max opened a drawer marked "1967," hoping it wasn't booby-trapped. It was crammed full of papers. He lifted one out and found it was a front page from the *Beacon*, but, rifling through, there were other newspapers too. The first headline read "74 dead in Russian Train

Derailment." He pulled out another: "Australian Prime Minister Lost Off Cheviot Beach."

"That's a bit careless," Max mumbled to himself.

"It's an archive," Kensy called from the other side of the room. "Like the one in the tower except that was mostly all about us." When she and Max had first arrived at Alexandria, they had discovered the tower and its contents but hadn't realized it was where their grandmother kept all of their cast-off clothes and copies of their school awards and reports and such.

"Yes," Max agreed. "The number on the drawer is the year. But I've only found front pages over here. Not just from the *Beacon* either. There are lots of different papers."

Kensy had discovered the same thing. Coincidentally, she was searching through the year she and Max were born. There was a headline about an avalanche in France and another about an oil spill off the coast of Alaska, but it was the third one she read that caused the girl to check herself. "Max, come here," she shouted. "Now!"

He quickly returned the papers to the drawer and hurried to his sister. She was holding a page from the *Times*. Emblazoned in large letters were the words "Newspaper Heir Killed in Plane Crash."

Max scanned the text. According to the story, his parents and Fitz had perished in a plane crash in the Andes. They were on holiday in Peru and their father was flying the private jet when the plane disappeared in mountainous terrain. Wreckage had been spotted and, once they could access it, bodies were likely to be recovered. Max read to the end of the report, then looked up. "Did you see this bit?" he said, pointing at the page. "Sadly, Anna Spencer's own parents, prominent medical scientists Hector and Marisol Clement, were murdered in a botched robbery last spring in their Paris home. A representative for Dame Cordelia Spencer has asked that the media respect the family's privacy at this terrible time."

Kensy's eyes widened. "Our grandparents

were *murdered*? Mum never mentioned *that*. Come to think of it, she's never really told us much about them."

"How do we even know it's true?" Max said. "After all, Mum and Dad and Fitz didn't die in a plane crash." He glanced at his watch. "We've got to go," he said, and returned the page to the drawer. "We're going to have to sprint back. If we're late, Vanden Boom will be having us for breakfast!"

The children made sure that nothing was out of place, then ran up the stairs. Max paused at the top, wondering how to reset the whole thing. As if sensing there was no one inside, the staircase retracted and the stone rumbled back into place of its own accord. Problem solved.

CHAPTER 6

COLODJE
Secets

The twins ran through the back door of the house and darted down the hall to the conservatory, where breakfast was being served. Several clocks chimed the half hour as they entered the room, red faced and puffing.

"Good morning, Maxim, Kensington," Romilly Vanden Boom greeted the pair. "Working on your fitness, were you? One hour and thirty minutes of exercise is impressive. Perhaps you could inspire others to be similarly motivated." The science teacher and gadgets expert eyeballed Alfie as he walked past. The lad's plate was piled high with scrambled eggs, bacon and a mountain of hash browns.

"Morning, mith," he mumbled, a rasher of bacon hanging from his mouth.

"Good heavens, Alfie. Your manners had better improve before Christmas dinner or Dame Spencer will banish you to eat in the piggery." Mrs. Vanden Boom shook her head. "Although the pigs might not appreciate your penchant for bacon," she added with a snigger.

"Thorry." Alfie grinned and carried on to his table.

Kensy cast her eyes around the room, hoping their uncle might join them, but there was no sign of him. She spotted Autumn, who already had her breakfast and was sitting at a table in the far corner with Carlos. She waved at the pair, then quickly helped herself to poached eggs on toast before making a beeline for their friends. Max waited, tray in hand, for Song to replenish the chafing dish of hash browns that Alfie had just emptied.

The butler hummed a country ditty as he worked. "You were out early this morning, Master Maxim," he commented.

The boy looked at Song, trying not to appear alarmed. "Kensy and I went for a run," he said, which wasn't exactly a lie. Clearly, from what Mrs. Vanden Boom said, someone had been monitoring their whereabouts.

"Did you see anything interesting?" Song asked.

"Not really," Max replied, dishing hash browns onto his plate. "Just sheep and fields."

He couldn't tell if it was his nerves, but Song's gaze seemed to linger on him for an extra beat longer than usual. Did the butler know more than he was letting on? If so, he'd likely tell their grandmother what they'd been up to. The last thing Max had intended to do when he woke up that morning was to get into trouble. The fact that they hadn't been sliced and diced either was a bonus, although now that Max thought about it, he'd forgotten to flick that switch back on again.

"Do not worry, Master Maxim," Song said with a smile. "I have taken care of things and your secret is safe with me."

Max looked at the man in astonishment. "Thanks," he whispered.

Unbeknownst to the boy, he was the object of someone else's close scrutiny. Autumn was eyeing Max from across the room. It was fast becoming a habit, despite her best efforts to conceal her feelings. "Where did you go this morning?" she asked as Kensy sat down.

"I bumped into Max in the hall and we decided to run along the cliffs," Kensy replied, chomping on her sourdough toast. The twins had agreed to keep this morning's discovery to themselves until they could learn more.

"Did you get to the lighthouse?" Carlos asked.

Kensy nodded. "Uh-huh."

"We'll have to show you the cave off the beach next time," Autumn said, exchanging a knowing grin with Carlos.

"Have you seen your uncle this morning?" Carlos inquired.

Kensy shook her head. "No, we only met

him for five minutes last night and then he disappeared by the time we'd finished the debriefing."

"So, what did you think?" Autumn said, resting her spoon in her bowl of porridge.

Kensy scratched her nose. "He certainly looks a lot like Dad and Max."

"Gorgeous, you mean," Autumn said dreamily. She turned bright red when she realized she'd said the words out loud.

Carlos made a gagging noise and Kensy almost choked. "Should I tell Uncle Rupert you've got a thing for him?" she teased. "Or Max?"

"What?" Autumn said, panicking. "No, I don't . . . They're just nice to look at, that's all."

Max slid into the seat across from his sister, wondering why Carlos and Kensy were grinning at him like mad hatters, and why Autumn's face resembled a tomato.

Carlos reached across and plucked a hash brown from Max's plate. "Thanks for saving me the trip."

"Good morning, children," Romilly Vanden Boom said over the chinking of cutlery. She waited for the din to die down. "This morning, each of you will be working on specific skills that your teachers have identified as areas requiring improvement." She pressed a button on the side of her watch and an image appeared against the white wall above the buffet.

Kensy scanned it for her name. "Max, we're learning to drive!" She clenched her fists with excitement.

"Great," Max said absently.

Carlos looked at the boy. "What's the matter with you? Last night you were practically begging me to take you to the racetrack and now Mrs. Vanden Boom might as well have said you were going to spend the morning massaging her bunions."

"Nothing, I'm fine," Max said, but in truth, his mind was still on the crypt and that article about his parents and grandparents. "Can't wait."

The previous evening, he had asked Carlos about their uncle's challenge to him and what it all meant. The lad had told him the estate had its own racetrack – a road circuit beyond the woods – concealed in an ingenious way, but had refused to tell him how. Max would have to see it for himself. When Carlos said they raced Formula Ford cars, Max had been over the moon.

"What have you been assigned?" Max asked.

"I'm on the archery range," Carlos griped. "Seriously, I can't believe my aim with a bow and arrow is even worse than with a gun."

Autumn had been assigned to high diving, which didn't thrill her terribly much either. She'd recently admitted to Kensy that she was crippled by a morbid fear of heights. The girl had tried her best to hide it from her teachers, but perhaps she hadn't concealed it as well as she'd thought.

The children were told to meet their instructors at the back door in fifteen minutes as their lessons were to be finished by lunchtime to prepare for the evening's festivities.

"Well, I know who'll be having the most fun this morning," Autumn said with a smile. "And guaranteed it won't be me or Carlos."

CHAPTER 7

⌐⊏∧⊡⊟⊙⟨⊐⌐ ⟨⟩⊓ȘₘₑRE⊡⟩ ⟨

The twins had driven to the racetrack with Mrs. Vanden Boom in one of the estate's numerous khaki Land Rovers. They were the only students undertaking driver training, as apparently the rest of them were all experts. The twins had both noticed that since arriving at Alexandria their science teacher had swapped her usual school attire of a white lab coat over an array of peasant skirts and floral blouses for sturdier outfits of jeans, Wellington boots and a Barbour jacket. She was looking far more relaxed than at school, where she was always rushing about.

"Mrs. Vanden Boom, can't people see the racetrack from the air?" Max asked. "And the noise must drive the neighbors mad. I remember we once went to Portugal and Estoril was just over the hill from where we were staying. Anytime you set foot outside, it sounded like millions of mosquitoes were about to attack."

Romilly smiled to herself. "Pharos has ways to make sure there are no prying eyes," the woman replied.

Kensy frowned. "The track's not covered by a roof or something, is it? Because that would be ridiculous *and* impossible."

Romilly's eyes flickered up to the rearview mirror and she grinned at the girl in the back seat. Kensy reminded her of herself as a child – constantly curious and always pulling things apart. Except that by her age Romilly had already built her first engine, right down to machining the parts. Her father had been in charge of all gadgets and technology for Pharos and was keen for Romilly to follow in his footsteps, but she loved teaching too.

Perhaps one day she'd make the change to full-time research and development, but for the moment life was just fine as it was. "You do know that everyone in the village and for miles surrounding us is part of Pharos, don't you?" Romilly said. "And your peers at school – their entire families as well, even if some are too young to understand it yet."

This was news to the twins although it made sense as Song had told them all the workers from the estate lived close by. About a mile from the ornate front gates of Alexandria was a gorgeous village of the same name. There were at least a dozen cottages, a pub called The Lamp and Lantern and a general store built around a village green. Several farmhouses bordered the enclave on the road to the main house. Max had seen some of the residents when they'd arrived, but he'd had no idea that it all belonged to his grandmother.

As they crested the top of the hill, Romilly stopped the car. Even after many years, she still thought the racetrack was one of the most brilliant things she'd ever seen. "There it is," she said.

Kensy leaned forward between the front seats. "Um, where?"

Max couldn't see anything other than a green field. "Is it a hologram?" he asked.

Romilly Vanden Boom smiled. "Largest one we've ever created."

"Mind officially blown," Kensy said, shaking her head as she sat back in her seat.

The Land Rover lurched forward and clattered along the road until they reached the track a half-mile further on. Carlos was right – it was a proper road circuit and the facilities wouldn't have looked out of place at Silverstone or Daytona.

The pit lane was deserted, and the row of garages seemed to be locked up tight. Perched in the middle of the squat row of sheds was a small tower that would have served as a commentary box at a commercial facility.

Max eyed the dented hatchback that was sitting on the edge of the roadway. "I thought we'd be driving Formula Ford cars."

"Yeah, so much for our race car lessons," Kensy grumbled.

Romilly Vanden Boom slapped her skinny thigh. "Has Rodriguez been filling your head with fanciful notions, Maxim?"

Max nodded. Learning to drive in a beaten-up yellow Fiesta wasn't at all what he'd had in mind.

Romilly directed the children to some changing rooms in the bottom of the tower. "You'll find your driving suits hanging up inside," the woman said.

"Is that really necessary?" Kensy asked. Puttering around the track would hardly require a special outfit.

Romilly Vanden Boom grinned. "I think you'll appreciate the need for your clothing once we get started."

Kensy and Max exchanged quizzical glances before disappearing into their respective changing rooms. They returned ten minutes later in fire-retardant racing suits, helmets, special leather boots and gloves. Kensy was decked out in blue and Max was in red.

Mrs. Vanden Boom was nowhere to be seen.

Suddenly, a voice bellowed from a loudspeaker and the children looked up to find their teacher inside the tower. She was wearing a headset and held a pair of binoculars in her left hand. "Right," she said, "Maxim, you're up first. Kensington, I want you in the passenger seat."

The children eyed the car on the edge of the track.

"Well, don't just stand there," the woman tutted. "Do you want to learn to drive or would you rather play tiddlywinks?"

The children made their way to the car and buckled their harnesses while Max checked if the key was in the ignition. Images popped up on the windshield, forming an instruction guide on how to start the car.

"You'll notice it's a manual transmission, so you'll have to learn how to change gears. There's a clutch on the left and next to it is the brake. The accelerator is on the right," Mrs. Vanden Boom's voice crackled through the headsets that were built into the twins' helmets. "Left leg for the clutch. Right leg for the other two. Have a little play with it. And, Max, adjust the seats and mirrors accordingly. Now, I want you to listen to Esmerelda – she's going to talk you through everything."

"Who's Esmerelda?" the twins asked in unison.

"Good morning, Master Maxim, Miss Kensington," a cheery voice spoke. "It's lovely to make your acquaintance and I do apologize for my appearance. I'm afraid I've had a rather rough time of it the past few years."

Kensy looked around the vehicle. "Esmerelda," she said slowly, "are you . . . the car?"

"Yes, Miss Kensington, I am indeed. In the next hour, you and your brother are going to become expert drivers. Guaranteed! I never thought I'd see the day that I got to teach the two of you. I taught your father a long time ago, and Agent Williams. I've had an update since then, but between you and me, I think I'm long overdue for another one – I've had a slew of overly enthusiastic learners of late, somewhat lacking in skills. Now, shall we begin?"

Max couldn't believe his ears. Since when were talking cars a thing? Then again, when did self-tying shoelaces with the ability to fly out of your shoes and turn into a lasso exist either?

Esmerelda gave Max blow-by-blow instructions on how to start the car, put it into gear, accelerate, change gears, steer and brake. He completed his first lap of the track with hardly a crunch.

"This is amazing!" The boy grinned. "I'm driving."

Kensy yawned theatrically. "Woo-hoo," she said, her voice dripping with sarcasm. "Great job, except I think I just saw Mrs. Thornthwaite overtake us with her shopping cart."

"Ouch, Kens. There's no need to be mean." Max pushed his foot down a little further on the accelerator.

"Miss Kensington, your brother is doing very well," Esmerelda said. After a pause, she added, "But, Master Maxim, I will advise that you step on it. I need you to do the next lap at sixty."

Max gulped. "Sixty kilometers an hour?"

"No, sixty *miles* per hour, Master Maxim," Esmerelda replied politely.

Max did the conversion in his head. "But that's one hundred kilometers an hour!"

"By the end of our session, I expect you to take a lap at almost twice that speed," Esmerelda said. "And don't take your eyes off the road. You never know what might jump out at you."

Kensy fidgeted in her seat, itching for her turn behind the wheel. She felt a rush of excitement and desperately wanted to show Esmerelda and Mrs. Vanden Boom that, out of the two of them, she was the better driver. Of course, she didn't actually know if that was the case, but she couldn't wait to give it a whirl.

Max tentatively increased speed just as they rounded a blind bend. Without warning, a flock of sheep filled their view.

"Max, look out!" Kensy screamed, throwing up her hands to shield herself.

Max swerved to the right, managing to miss the sheep that had appeared out of nowhere.

Esmerelda talked him through the gear changes and how to avoid spinning out.

"Were they real?" Kensy asked, her nerves jangling as Max pressed his foot to the floor on the long straight. He watched the speedometer climb until it hovered at one hundred and twenty. It felt like they were flying.

"Well done, Master Maxim," Esmerelda said. "Please drive into the pits and change over. I am looking forward to seeing what your sister can do. As for the sheep, yes, of course they were real. Where do you think I got all these dents from? And I'm afraid those red marks on the tarmac aren't tomato sauce."

Kensy's prediction was right and she soon proved herself, setting a cracking pace around the track and earning great praise from Esmerelda and Mrs. Vanden Boom.

"Last lap," Esmerelda reminded her. "Now, I really want you to go for it!"

Without a moment's hesitation, Kensy slammed the pedal to the floor, changing through the gears as she reached the top of the long straight. She braked hard as they neared the first set of chicanes, successfully negotiating the bends, then rapidly increased her speed as they crested up and over the hill. The Fiesta shot across the finish line.

"Told you I'd beat your time!" Kensy said triumphantly. "Ha!"

"Keep your hair on, Kens. I noticed there were no stray flocks of sheep on any of your laps," Max retorted.

Kensy eased her foot off the accelerator and gently pressed the brake. When the Fiesta failed to respond, she pressed the pedal harder. Again, nothing happened. "Um, Max," she said, fighting the panic rising in her throat, "the brakes . . . aren't working."

In fact, despite pumping her foot up and down on the pedal, the car was only going faster. It was then that the twins realized Esmerelda had been strangely silent since they'd started the last lap.

"Mrs. Vanden Boom!" Max shouted into his headset. "We have no brakes and Esmerelda's not answering!"

There was no reply from their teacher either.

Kensy held tight to the steering wheel as the hatchback flew over the top of the hill. When they landed with a jolting thud, the car swerved sharply to the left. Kensy tugged at the wheel with all her might, trying to correct it, but it jerked away from her, as if possessed. The Fiesta veered left and right so violently that the twins were thrown against the doors.

"Pull the hand brake!" Max shouted as they were flung from side to side. The boy's helmet smacked against the window.

Kensy reached for the lever between them. She didn't know what to expect, but, given they were heading straight for a concrete barrier, she had little choice. "Here goes nothing!" she yelled, yanking the hand brake as hard as she could.

The car was thrown into a spin. Around and around and around it went, like an out-of-control carousel, before slamming sideways into one of the barriers, teetering on two wheels and then crashing back down onto the track.

For a moment, the whole world fell silent. It was as if they were in a state of suspended animation.

"Are you okay?" Kensy panted.

Max nodded. A blanket of white steam poured from under Esmerelda's hood. Through the cracked windshield, Kensy spotted the Land Rover hurtling down the hill toward them. Romilly pulled up beside Esmerelda and leapt from the car.

"Thank goodness you're alive!" she gasped, wrenching Kensy's door open. She released the girl's harness and dragged her from the wreckage.

Max unbuckled his seat belt and crawled across to the driver's side. His own door was jammed against the barrier. As he clambered onto the ground, he felt a splash against his right hand. He raised it to his nose and coughed, the pungent odor immediately recognizable. Max pushed himself to his feet and took off toward Romilly and Kensy, who was now in the back seat of the Land Rover.

"Mrs. Vanden Boom! The fuel tank is leaking!" he called, pointing to the pool of liquid that was slowly trickling closer to her and Kensy.

Romilly ran around to the front of the car just in time to see a spark ignite at the rear of the Fiesta.

The flame flickered to life, licking at Esmerelda's battered panels. "She's going to blow," Max said in horror.

Kensy opened the back door of the Land Rover. "Max! My watch – it's gone. It must have fallen off in the car when we crashed."

Tears fell onto the tops of the girl's cheeks. Max's mind raced.

"Oh, no, you don't!" Romilly yelled, but the boy wasn't to be stopped.

He ran back across the tarmac and dove into the car as the flames danced around it. Romilly Vanden Boom ripped an extinguisher from under the dashboard of the Land Rover and raced toward the burning Fiesta, spraying it with foam. Still, the flames intensified.

"Max!" Kensy screamed as the fire took hold. "Get out of there!"

Her chest tightened as she spied her brother's silhouette surrounded by fire and then, finally, he was running at them. His suit was intact, and he was holding something in his hand. Romilly doused Max with foam and grabbed his arm, the pair charging toward the Land Rover. She bundled him into the front and jumped into the driver's seat, turning the ignition and planting her foot on the accelerator as Esmerelda exploded, sending a fireball hurtling into the sky.

Perched on the edge of the topmost diving board, Autumn was willing herself to remain calm. She squeezed her eyes shut, took a deep breath and was about to launch into the air, when there was a loud bang. The diving board shook beneath her feet, throwing the girl off balance. Autumn managed to steady herself and looked out in time to see a burst of red in the sky. She scurried back to the railing and gripped it, seized by a fear that stemmed beyond her phobia of heights.

At the archery range, Carlos saw it too. His breath caught in his throat as he lowered his weapon. If he was right, the plume of black smoke was coming from the racetrack.

CHAPTER 8

EWAO JJEVOOE

Kensy reached forward from the back seat to touch her brother's arm. "You could have been killed," she said.

Max squeezed her hand and smiled. "But I wasn't and, here, I got your watch," he said, passing it back to her.

She received it with shaking hands and held on to it tightly, not trusting herself to put it on again just yet.

"Well, thank heavens for those suits is all I can say," Romilly Vanden Boom declared as she drove them to the pits while the inferno that was Esmerelda raged unchallenged.

A garage door opened and she steered inside what appeared at first glance to be a mobile medical center. Romilly hopped out of the car and retrieved a device that resembled a flashlight from a locked cupboard. "You'll need to hop out and put this on so you're not affected by the light," the woman instructed, handing Kensy an eye mask.

Once Kensy did as she was bid, Mrs. Vanden Boom told her to hold out her arms as she flicked a switch on the cylindrical instrument and pointed it at the girl. A hologram of Kensy appeared beside her. The teacher examined the image, bringing up the statistics on Kensy's heart rate, blood pressure, brain function and various other faculties. When she was satisfied that nothing was amiss, Romilly switched it off and the image disappeared back into the tube.

"Whoa – that's incredible. I just saw your heart beating and the blood flowing through your veins," Max said.

"Yes, we find the RUOK 4.0 very handy, particularly when assessing injuries in the field," Romilly said, handing Max his own mask and giving him the once-over. When the woman was finished, she stepped back. "You're both fine, although, Kensington, you've suffered quite a shock. And, Max, what were you thinking? It's only a watch. I know it's special, but we could have gotten Kensy another – perhaps not exactly the same but close."

"No, we couldn't!" Kensy blurted. She glanced away from the quizzical look on their teacher's face. "Mum and Dad gave it to me for my birthday," she added softly.

"Ah, I see." Romilly punched a couple of buttons on the side of the device. She peered at the screen intently.

"Has Esmerelda ever done anything like that before?" Max asked.

Romilly shook her head. "Not to my knowledge. There will be a full investigation, and we should be able to get the data from the black-box recorder. Hopefully we'll find out exactly what happened. Kensington, you did an amazing job – the speed you were going . . . Well, let's just say there could have been a very different outcome."

A few sips of water and a honey sandwich procured from a cooler in the Land Rover seemed to have a restorative effect on the girl. Kensy's mind went from numb to churning in seconds.

"I think Esmerelda tried to kill us," Kensy stated. "Lucky we got her first."

"That isn't possible," Mrs. Vanden Boom said firmly. "Her technology is state of the art. I suspect there has been human intervention."

"So, *someone else* tried to kill us," the girl said, reeling at the prospect. "Great."

Romilly thought for a moment. It certainly did appear that way. She directed the children back into the car and returned the RUOK 4.0 to its drawer.

Kensy looked at her brother. "I wish Fitz was here."

"Me too," the boy replied. Maybe, by some miracle, Fitz would find their parents and they'd all be home for Christmas. Even

Max wasn't immune to the odd fanciful notion.

"Do you think this could have had anything to do with those headlights we saw going over the hill before dawn?" Kensy whispered. "When I ended up in Miss Witherbee's room last night, she was talking on the phone and told whoever it was not to worry and that Shugs was on it first thing. What if it was him – again?"

"We have no proof that it was Shugs in the first place. Whoever did this must have known we were on driver training today," Max said. "We can't go around accusing Miss Witherbee or Shugs until we have some evidence."

Kensy slumped in her seat and folded her arms. "I hate that you're right," she said, much to her brother's surprise.

The children hushed as Romilly hopped in behind the wheel.

Kensy leaned forward in her seat. "Mrs. Vanden Boom, do you think we could keep this quiet for now – at least the bit about the sabotage? I know you have to tell Granny, but the kids don't need to know, do they?"

Romilly started the engine. "Of course. I'm sure your grandmother will leave no stone unturned looking for the culprit."

"You can just tell everyone Kensy's a terrible driver and that poor old Esmerelda came off second best," Max said, garnering a glare from his sister.

"Don't worry," Romilly said, "I'll get Esmerelda – or whatever's left of her – locked up tight. Perhaps you're right about a cover – although Kensy is a magnificent driver."

Kensy grinned at Max. "Yeah, we might have to tell everyone it was you driving. It'll be more believable."

Romilly drove the children to the house, where they were met by Song at the back door. He'd cleared the decks, making sure they could get upstairs without any questions. As was to be expected, the explosion had caused a fuss and there had already been quite a bit of speculation.

"Miss Kensington, Master Maxim, I am pleased to see that you are both in one piece," the man said as he helped Kensy from the car. "Confucius says by three methods we may learn wisdom. First by reflection, which is the noblest; second by imitation, which is the easiest; and third by experience, which is the bitterest. It sounds as though you have experienced number three."

The poor girl was still shaking. Song led the way upstairs, but instead of turning left toward their bedrooms he turned right.

"Where are we going?" Max asked.

"Dame Spencer has requested you use her suite to get some rest. The house is getting busier and her wing is very quiet. I have organized some clothes for you both, and may I suggest a bath? It might help settle your nerves." The man continued to the end of the hall and gave a perfunctory knock on the door before pushing it open.

The trio was greeted by Wellie and Mac, who danced excitedly at their feet. Sitting in front of the window was a beautifully decorated Christmas tree, the smell of its pine needles filling the room.

Dame Spencer was downstairs greeting the guests with the assistance of Song's twin brother, Sidney, her city butler. He had arrived earlier from London.

"I will be back shortly with some soup." Song bowed and exited.

"I call having a bath first," Kensy said, and promptly disappeared.

Max sunk down onto one of the couches, exhausted by his mind replaying the lead-up to the accident in an infernal loop. "There has to be a double agent – someone working for Pharos who, for whatever reason, wants us dead," he mumbled to himself. "But why? What have we done?"

The events of the morning sat like a brick on his chest. He closed his eyes for just a moment. When he opened them, his nostrils twitched at the smell of pumpkin soup. There was a steaming bowl sitting in front of him on the coffee table. Kensy was on the other couch, dressed in a tracksuit, her hair wrapped in a white towel atop her head.

"How long have I been asleep?" Max asked, sitting up and discreetly wiping the trickle of drool that had collected on his chin.

"Half an hour," she said, and pointed to the left side of her mouth. "I think you missed a bit."

Max stretched and stood up, walking to the window where a steady stream of cabs was puttering up the driveway, delivering the rest of the guests. Mr. Nutting was back in PE-teacher mode, refereeing a vigorous game of football on the lower lawn beyond the Atlas fountain. Every now and then one of the children would peel off to greet their parents.

Max turned away from the scene. "What do you make of that headline about our grandparents?"

Kensy shrugged and slurped her soup. "Mum never said anything about her parents being murdered. I suppose she might've been trying to protect us – if it's true."

"We should do some research." Max glanced around the room, wondering if by any chance his grandmother had a laptop lying about.

"Or ask Song or Mim – they might tell us," Kensy said.

There was a knock on the door and Mim poked her head inside. Unusually for her, the woman's gray hair was pulled back into a loose bun instead of snaking down her back in a long plait. She'd swapped her customary overalls and Wellington boots for a pretty floral dress. "Hello," she said, walking in. "I hear you two have had quite the adventure this morning. Are you all right?"

The twins nodded. When she'd had her bath earlier, Kensy had noticed some red marks that were likely to turn into bruises on her right shoulder, and she imagined her brother would be black-and-blue on his left arm given how hard he'd smashed against the side of the car, but at least there was nothing on their faces. For all intents and purposes, they both looked perfectly fine.

"Have you heard from Fitz?" Kensy asked.

"No, but I'm sure he'll check in later," the woman said. She perched on the arm of the chair beside the girl.

"Mim, can we ask you something?" Max said.

"Yes, of course," Mim replied, "but that doesn't mean I'll know the answer."

"Were Mum's parents really murdered in a botched robbery?"

Mim brushed her hair off her face. "Who told you that?"

"We saw something – and we don't know if it's true because Mum never said anything to us about it," the boy explained.

Mim nodded slowly. "It was a terrible business. They were wonderful people."

Kensington felt her stomach drop. She left the last spoonful of her soup and put the bowl down on the coffee table. "You knew them?"

Mim stared ahead as if thinking about something. "Only a little."

"What were they like?" Kensy asked.

"Lovely. Terribly clever and both very funny. Your grandfather, Hector, was a gifted storyteller and your grandmother, Marisol, was quite possibly the most elegant woman I've ever known. She could make a lab coat look like couture," Mim mused.

"Were they part of *this* too?" Max asked. He waved his hands around the room.

"Oh, no, your mother wasn't born into Pharos — she married into the organization, same as Cordelia," Mim said. "Cordelia was a young journalist working at the paper. She was a feisty girl — so determined to succeed in what was back then very much a man's world. You remind me a lot of her, Kensy. She'd earned herself a scholarship to study at Oxford and had made quite the journey from her home in Sydney all the way to England. Anyway, she and my brother fell madly in love and the rest is history."

Max frowned as he remembered something. "Mrs. Grigsby at the newsagency in London told us that Granny Cordelia's parents were killed — run over by a bus, I think she said. Is that true?"

Mim paused before answering. "I'm afraid we never really got to the bottom of it. It was a terrible tragedy and just so unlikely."

The twins looked at each other in alarm. There was so much about their family they didn't yet know, and surely that was one too many accidents for it to be mere coincidence.

"Did Mum's parents know about Dad and what he did?" Kensy asked.

"As far as your grandparents were concerned, your father was a newspaper man, like my brother had been."

Max flinched. "Was he?" All their lives the children had thought their father was a paramedic, but of course that could have been his cover once he and their mother left the organization.

"Your father was – *is* – a very clever man. He met your mother at university, where they were both studying medicine, but then your grandmother needed him and he put his medical ambitions on hold and ended up working at the paper with her."

"So, Mum took after her parents except it said they were medical scientists," Max said. "What sort of research were they involved in?"

Mim put her hand on Kensy's shoulder. "I'm afraid I don't know anything more."

Kensy looked at the woman, a wave of emotion rolling over her. No matter how hard she tried to stop them, tears filled her eyes.

"Oh, sweetheart." The woman opened her arms and Kensy tumbled into them.

"I just want Mum and Dad to come home," the girl sobbed. "I miss them so much."

Max's eyes began to prickle. Mim looked at the boy and beckoned for him to join them. She wrapped an arm around him too. "My darlings, have faith in that son of mine," she said, hugging them tight. "He'll do everything he can to find them. I know it."

CHAPTER 9

ᒥᔭ᙭᙭ ᙓᐁᗡᒧᔭᗡᗡᘓ

"So, ugly sweaters for Christmas are a big thing in England, are they?" Kensy reread the instructions attached to the beautifully printed card sitting on her bedside table.

Autumn nodded and struck a pose. Her red sweater featured a reindeer face with three-dimensional antlers and a bulbous nose. "Do you actually think I'd wear this special little number if I didn't have to?"

Kensy laughed. "Okay, that's truly hideous, and I'm pretty sure it's exactly the same as the one hanging in my wardrobe in London.

I wish I'd known. I could have brought it with me."

"Oh, don't worry. There's one for you here somewhere." Autumn hurried into the walk-in closet and appeared a few seconds later, holding up another red monstrosity. This sweater had a Christmas tree adorned with three-dimensional ornaments and lights.

Kensy laughed. "It's worse than yours. I didn't think that was even possible five minutes ago."

"And I suspect it's going to get more interesting the longer you wear it," Autumn added, wiggling her eyebrows.

"Those lights don't actually work, do they?" Kensy grimaced. She was feeling much better since having a rest and something to eat. Cordelia had come to see how she and Max were feeling and said that everyone had been briefed on the accident and told not to bring it up. Their grandmother had stressed the fact that they shouldn't worry about it. Anyway, the twins had decided to try to enjoy the first Christmas of their strange new lives regardless.

Autumn had arrived at Kensy's room after catching up with her parents. They had just flown in from Hong Kong, where they headed up the Southeast Asian bureau of Pharos – the reason Autumn lived with an aunt in London. Apart from giving Kensy an unexpected hug, Autumn hadn't mentioned a thing about what had happened at the racetrack. Clearly, she was incredibly relieved to find her friend in one piece. Carlos had been similarly accommodating with Max next door. The boy hadn't even cracked a joke about it.

Kensy changed into jeans, boots and a long-sleeved T-shirt and pulled her sweater over the top. Autumn went into the bathroom to check her hair as a knock sounded on the door.

"Come in if you're good-looking!" Kensy yelled.

Max stepped into the room.

"What are you doing here? I said come in if you're good-looking." Kensy made a face and giggled. She didn't see Autumn steal a glance at the boy from the bathroom doorway and suppress the smile that was tickling her lips.

"What? You don't think I look . . ." Max spun around like a model on a catwalk, planting his left hand on his hip. "Chic?"

Kensy and Autumn burst out laughing. Max's sweater was even worse than theirs.

"Is that Wellie and Mac on there?" Kensy asked. The dogs' faces embroidered onto it bore a remarkable resemblance to their grandmother's West Highland terriers.

"Sure is." Max patted the tops of their heads. "It's always good to have a Westie on your chesty."

Kensy cringed and shook her head. "That is wrong on every level."

"As if you can talk," Max retorted, pointing to the ornaments on her sweater, which had begun to glow. "Also, aren't you forgetting something?"

Kensy looked down. "What do you mean? I've got pants on."

"Would it hurt you to run a brush through that shrubbery you call hair every once in a while?" He looked to Autumn for support, but the girl just blushed.

Kensy rolled her eyes. "All right, Mum," she said, and a pang of guilt hit her in the chest like a thump with a wet sock.

"I could braid it," Autumn offered. "I'm really fast."

Kensy shot past her and into the bathroom to grab a brush and a hair band. She wasn't going to think about her mum and dad and Fitz. They were fine. They had to be; there was no other option.

Max smiled at Autumn. "Kensy's lucky to have you as a friend."

Autumn's lashes flickered as she lowered her eyes. She could feel the heat rising up her neck to her cheeks. An awkward silence hung in the air between them.

"I'd better check on Carlos," the lad said, as his sister bounded back into the room and tossed the brush to Autumn.

The girl reached out and caught it like a seasoned fielder on the cricket team.

"We'll wait for you at the top of the stairs," Max said.

"See you soon," Autumn replied, her eyes

lingering on the boy as he departed.

Kensy sat at the dressing table and Autumn set to work. True to her word, she had the girl's wild blonde locks tamed and woven into a fishbone braid in less than two minutes.

"Wow, that looks amazing," Kensy said, admiring her reflection in the mirror. "Maybe you should teach me – although, really, I can't imagine I'd have the patience."

Autumn grinned at her friend in the mirror. "It's dead easy once you get the hang of it."

"Come on," Kensy said, jumping to her feet, "or we'll be late and I don't even know where the ballroom is."

"Prepare to be amazed, Kensington Grey!" Autumn declared, and the pair of them raced off to join in the fun.

CHAPTER 10

LNᗡᒋᒷᓄ∧ᒐᒷ ᗡ𝖥ᗡ

As Kensy and Max soon discovered, there was a whole other wing to the house they hadn't yet explored and a huge part of it was taken up by the ballroom. The children were greeted at the double doors by Dame Spencer, who was wearing a navy skirt paired with a red sweater that played host to three cheeky squirrels emblazoned across the front.

"Hello, darlings," she said with a smile. "Don't you all look splendid!"

Max glanced inside the room. To his great relief and amusement, everyone was wearing something equally awful, adding to the feeling of fun in the air. That, and the upbeat Christmas song that was playing.

"There's plenty to eat and drink," Cordelia added, pointing to the buffet table, which was being guarded on either end by life-sized nutcrackers. "It's help yourselves tonight as all of the staff are officially off duty. Enjoy every minute and make sure to reserve a spot on your dance cards for me."

Kensy grinned as she caught sight of Song in a sweater that featured Santa wearing a cowboy hat on the front. Sidney's sweater, meanwhile, was resplendent with a picture of Elvis dressed as an elf.

As ornate as it was large, the ballroom was decorated with white paneling on the lower half of the walls and flocked crimson wallpaper above. The ceiling's intricate plaster-work resembled the icing on a wedding cake, adorned with a central crystal chandelier, while a crackling fire danced in the hearth of the vast marble fireplace at the end of the room. Fairy lights added to the festive atmosphere and there were life-sized tin soldiers in addition to the nutcrackers standing sentry along the walls. A majestic fir tree stood in the middle of the room. Curiously, not a single ornament or string of tinsel hung from its branches.

"The tree's a bit bare compared to the rest of it," Max commented.

"Wait and see," Carlos said. "It's all part of the fun."

Autumn nodded. "It's my favorite part of Christmas at Alexandria."

Kensy and Max were intrigued. For the next hour or so, the children mingled with their friends and in turn met lots of the parents too, although some of them they already knew. Sachin's mother and father ran a curry house on Brick Lane in East London, where Song and Fitz had taken the twins for dinner a couple of times, and Kensy had been for a sleepover at Harper's home in Chelsea. Max had gone with Song to pick her up and met the family as well.

They both found it slightly off-putting that many of the adults seemed quite teary in their presence, concerned for the children's welfare in the wake of their parents' disappearance. Everyone asked how they were feeling and if they were okay. It wasn't making the situation any easier, although Kensy and Max did their best to smile through it. Mrs. Trimm's husband, Hayward, had hugged Max so tightly the boy thought he might suffocate. Elva had to nudge the man three times before he released the lad.

"It's absolutely wonderful to meet you both," Hayward effused. He was a long streak of a fellow with a bald patch on the back of his head in a perfect circle. Despite being follicle challenged up top, he had a splendid beard and moustache that he obviously took great pride in.

Kensy spotted Mrs. Varma glimmering like a Christmas ornament among the crowd and hurried over to say hello. The woman was bejeweled from head to toe in a glittering green sari, which she had teamed with a cardigan covered in sequined snowflakes.

"What fun!" she exclaimed, hugging Kensy and then Autumn. "I love Christmas – it's just so . . . twinkly."

Beside them, Max and Carlos had caught up with Sachin and his father and were now engaged in a fiery debate about the Ashes cricket tour of Australia. Mr. Varma was determined the English would win despite a first-test loss. Max felt a little torn in his allegiances, given his grandmother was Australian and it was the most recent country he had lived in before coming to the UK. In many ways, he felt far more Australian than English.

Mrs. Varma excused herself to go and speak with the Ahmeds, who had arrived a moment ago. Kensy spied Misha Thornhill standing in the far corner of the room and guided Autumn over to say hello.

"Hey, are you okay?" Kensy asked.

"Golly, I must look like a complete dweeb over here on my own." Misha smiled tightly. "I was just running something through my head."

Autumn's brow crinkled with concern. "Are you close to a breakthrough with the Lemmlers?"

"I think so," Misha said. "I can't help feeling sorry for Lola. Even though she's ghastly, I'm afraid life is going to be tricky for her when things unravel. She thinks her father is a saint, although I suppose most kids do, don't they? You know, his name's not even Lemmler. It's Leonardi. I can't say much more, but I'll let you know when things are about to heat up. I suspect it might be soon."

When the twins had first started at Central London Free School, Kensy had immediately come up against the resident bully, Lola Lemmler. Her best friend, Misha Thornhill, seemed to be her closest ally and it was often said that Misha didn't have an original thought unless Lola told her so. However, when the existence of the spy school was revealed, Kensy and Max also learned that Misha had merely been playing a part in an undercover operation. She was tasked with befriending Lola to get close to the girl's father, who was suspected to be a big player in organized crime. Kensy and Max had been stunned to see Misha down in Pharos headquarters, located beneath their school, the day they learned what was really going on.

It had taken Kensy a while to come to

grips with the fact that Misha was actually quite lovely away from Lola – but they all had to continue playing their roles at school. It was fortunate Misha was an extremely good actress. Kensy told her she should think about a career on stage when she finished school, but apparently the girl was keen on molecular biology and thought she'd be of more use to the organization planted in a science laboratory somewhere.

"I like your outfit," Autumn said. Misha's pink crocheted sweater boasted a pretty pattern of dainty candy canes. It even gave off a faint peppermint scent. "You smell quite delicious."

Misha grinned. "It's not the ugliest I've ever worn," she conceded, "but it means I won't stand a chance in the competition. You know how Mr. MacGregor loves the truly awful ones. Besides, my 'bestie' wouldn't allow me to be seen dead in anything as gross as yours."

Kensy glanced around the room and realized there were a lot of people she didn't know. Then again, Pharos couldn't have solely consisted of the teachers and students.

The unfamiliar faces must have belonged to field agents or people who worked behind the scenes. Kensy felt a twinge of excitement thinking about the future that lay ahead for her and Max, which was somewhat tempered when she noticed Shugs and O'Leary talking to Miss Witherbee on the other side of the room. Finally, this was her chance. She excused herself and marched toward the trio.

All three had entered into the spirit of the occasion clad in equally unattractive sweaters. Mr. O'Leary's sported a leprechaun dressed as Santa Claus, while Shugs's was similar to Kensy's. Miss Witherbee had a snowman with a lifelike carrot nose. The woman beamed at the girl over the top of her champagne flute.

"Hello, Kensy. Did you have a good day?" she asked before taking a sip.

"I'm sure you've heard *all* about my day," Kensy replied with an exaggerated wink. "After all, you helped plan it, didn't you?"

Willow Witherbee choked on her champagne while the two men looked completely bewildered. "Whatever do you mean?" she sputtered.

"I thought you organized for Mr. Shugs to do something first thing?" Kensy said.

"How on earth did you know that?" The woman pouted. "Your uncle will be so sad that the surprise has been spoiled. He was terribly excited about giving you and Max your own race cars."

Kensy looked at her blankly. Well, she'd gotten that wrong, hadn't she? She was glad Max wasn't around to say "I told you so."

Willow downed the rest of her drink and wiggled her empty glass. "Think I'll get a refill," she said sweetly, and strode away.

Kensy turned toward Shugs and O'Leary. "Hello," she said as brightly as she could manage.

"'Appy Christmas, Miss Kensington," Mr. O'Leary replied in an Irish lilt. His words were sung more than spoken.

"'Appy Christmas, miss," Shugs echoed in his gravelly voice.

"I'm surprised I haven't met you both properly before now," Kensy said. "I remember you were moving the straw mannequins the first time Max and I came to Alexandria.

I thought you were talking about real bodies and then you were staring at me in the greenhouse. You scared me half to death."

The pair grinned and nodded sheepishly. "We didn't mean to frighten you, pet," Mr. O'Leary apologized. "I suppose we've been given to staring because we never thought we'd see the day you and your brother were 'ere. It's made Dame Spencer the 'appiest we've seen 'er in years. She put on a good show and all that, but you can see it in 'er eyes. She's positively glowin'."

"We both knew your dad when 'e was a younger lad. Your bruvver is the spittin' image of 'im," Shugs added.

The more the man spoke the more Kensy couldn't get the thought out of her mind that it was him who had tried to kidnap them in London in the back of the taxi. Problem was, he didn't look anything like that fellow. And how she was ever going to prove it was anyone's guess. "Do you have any brothers, Mr. Shugs?" she asked.

The man shook his head. "No, just me," he replied, visibly puzzled by the question.

Mr. O'Leary chuckled. "Miss Kensington, you surely 'aven't seen another fella as ugly as this bloke 'ere."

Shugs scoffed. "You're not exactly a pinup yourself, old man."

"I'd better go and find my brother," Kensy said. She flashed them a smile before hurrying away. Just being close to Shugs gave her the heebie-jeebies.

Despite the smiles, Paddy O'Leary couldn't help feeling there was more to the girl's question. He hoped Shugs wasn't up to no good. Unfortunately, it wouldn't be the first time.

The Christmas music that had been playing in the background faded to the sound of Dame Spencer tapping a teaspoon against a cut-crystal tumbler. The crowd hushed and formed a semicircle around the woman.

"Good evening, friends and family," she began. "I'd like to formally welcome you all to our annual Christmas celebrations at Alexandria – a time when we can come together and pay our respects to the traditions of all our members. Tonight will mean many different things for everyone, but, for me, most of all it means family." She smiled at Kensy and Max, her eyes sparkling. "I never thought I'd see the day when . . ."

A loud ruckus at the double doors caused everyone to turn. The crowd parted to make way for a rather flushed and disheveled Rupert Spencer. He wore a white turtleneck imprinted with a photograph of his mother's face. A tiara embellished with diamanté sat atop her head and the words "ice queen" were stitched below the portrait.

Max and Kensy looked at one another.

"Hello, Mummy," Rupert drawled, raising a glass of champagne into the air. "Sorry I'm late. Got caught up at The Lamp and Lantern – intense game of pool with some out-of-towners. Did I miss anything important?"

Mim sighed loudly and shook her head at Cordelia, whose cheeks seemed to drain of their color. "Rupert," she said quietly, "please let your mother speak. I'm sure that you can have the stage in a little while."

"Is he . . . drunk?" Kensy whispered.

"I hope so, or else it means he's just plain rude," Max whispered back.

"Good evening, darling." Dame Spencer ignored her son's antics and continued her speech. "As I was about to say, I never thought I'd see the day when my grandchildren were able to be part of our celebrations. I only wish Edward and Anna were here with us too. And Fitz, of course. But I'm confident they will all be back soon."

"Hear, hear!" Rupert cried, jabbing his glass toward her. He thrust it forth with such force that a small wave of champagne splattered the crowd.

Mr. Varma mopped the back of his neck with his handkerchief while the rest of the room glared in Rupert's direction. Several partygoers muttered that he should jolly well pipe down.

Cordelia cleared her throat and took a deep breath. "But for now, let us celebrate all things good in the world. Christmas is a time to give thanks for our family and friends, our prosperity and opportunity to serve and protect our fellow man. Maxim, Kensington, would you come and join me, please?"

The twins hesitated for a few seconds before Mim gave them each a gentle nudge. Max reached for his sister's hand and the pair walked into their grandmother's open arms.

"Fwee cheers for Kenthy and Math," a muffled voice declared.

Kensy and Max both laughed from where they were now standing, on either side of their grandmother. Mr. Reffell was known for dressing in character to teach their lessons and tonight he had outdone himself. Although he wasn't wearing a sweater, the man's entire body was encased by a knitted snowman onesie.

"Oh, Monty, you goose," Elva Trimm, the school dinner lady and poisons and explosives specialist, called out, to great guffaws. Soon, a rousing chorus echoed around the room in celebration of the family reunion.

But there was something else brewing. Autumn had spied Mr. MacGregor inching his way toward the back of the crowd, joining Mr. Nutting and Miss Witherbee, who were doing the same thing. The three of them disappeared right in the middle of Dame Spencer's speech.

Max had spotted them too. He raised an eyebrow at Autumn, who shrugged her shoulders. He also noticed several other adults speaking into their sleeves and casting odd looks across the room. Whatever was happening clearly couldn't wait.

Cordelia, on the other hand, was either oblivious or intentionally ignoring what was going on. "Well, I think we should get the celebrations underway," she declared. "First, we'd better announce this year's ugly sweater winner, before Mr. Reffell faints from heat exhaustion. Then, my dear friends, it's time to trim the tree!"

CHAPTER 11

⌐ ⌐⌐⌐⌐⌐⌐⌐ ⌐⌐⌐⌐

Autumn and Carlos had been right when they said that Christmas at Alexandria would be like nothing Kensy and Max had ever experienced. They were happy that Mr. Reffell won the ugly sweater competition hands down – anyone who was prepared to suffer under that much itchy wool deserved it.

The guests who had disappeared earlier materialized once again and were enjoying the celebrations while Rupert had become the life of the party, seemingly forgiven for his previous indiscretions as he roamed through the crowd, smiling and laughing.

Decorating the tree was something to behold. A beautiful sleigh, chock-full of ornaments of every shape and size, was pulled into the room by Wellie and Mac. The pair wore little coats that made them look like miniature reindeer and had hoods with antlers too. The twins thought the whole thing impossible, really, as the sleigh was far too big and heavy for the two dogs. It had to have some sort of self-propulsion. Kensy immediately began to investigate, but was diverted back to the tree by Max when it was their turn to add ornaments.

Music played in the background while guests scaled ladders to the higher boughs. The crowning star was put in place by Dante Moretti, who had been bestowed the honor by Dame Spencer for his outstanding work during the year. Strapped into a harness, the boy descended through a hole in the ceiling to delicately position the jeweled ornament on the very top of the tree. He then whizzed along an invisible zip line back to the floor.

Kensy loved seeing her teachers with their families. Mr. MacGregor's wife, Tippie, was fabulously glam with cascading blonde curls and a slash of red lipstick. She wore a miniskirt, long boots and a simple white sweater adorned with mistletoe around the scalloped neckline. The way the couple looked at one another like love-struck teenagers reminded Kensy of her parents.

Mr. Nutting's wife, Emily, was the epitome of calm and collected as she dealt with their five children under the age of seven. Nothing seemed to worry her – when the youngest spilt milk down her front, she dabbed the spot dry; when their twin boys decided to play frisbee with a plate, she intercepted it and sent them off on a treasure hunt. Kensy was equally impressed with Mr. Nutting's kid-wrangling skills. There hadn't been a tear or tantrum all night, although the man did spend the majority of the time on the floor covered in children.

When the karaoke machine was wheeled out, Song and Sidney took to the stage and engaged in a serious contest. Song belted out a country version of "Here Comes Santa Claus," which was swiftly followed up with his brother's performance of "Winter Wonderland" in the tradition of his idol, Elvis Presley. The trouble was, singing wasn't either man's forte. Mr. Reffell, still in costume and euphoric from having won the competition, had the crowd in stitches when he called out loudly, "Whoth thrangling the cat?"

Later in the evening, the Christmas tunes gave way to a more varied song sheet and that's when things got interesting. Dame Spencer was the first to hit the dance floor, shimmying and shaking with the vigor of a woman half her age. Rupert asked Kensy to dance and swung the girl around like a rag doll. She couldn't remember laughing so much in ages; when Mr. MacGregor and Mr. Rodriguez led the macarena, Kensy thought her sides were going to split – especially when they jumped in the wrong direction and sent each other flying across the room.

The grand finale was nothing short of spectacular. A well-known Michael Jackson tune began to thump from the speakers, summoning the teachers and parents to the floor for a Thriller-esque dance off – the two sides acting more like a bunch of street gangs than responsible secret agents. When Alfie joined in, displaying far more rhythm than one might have expected, everyone else got up and soon it was parents versus children versus teachers versus the rest of the merry crowd. Mr. O'Leary pulled some impressive moves out of the bag, while Shugs stood in the corner, citing a bum knee.

When the clock struck eleven, Song clapped his hands and the music stopped. Dame Spencer thanked her guests for a wonderful evening. It was Christmas in less than an hour and the children had better be fast asleep before midnight, lest Santa bypass Alexandria. Mrs. Nutting had already disappeared with three of their children, but her husband was busily trying to extricate the twins from under the Christmas tree.

"But we want to see Santa," they complained.

Daphne Potts, the headmaster's personal assistant, used her excellent negotiation skills to talk them out, saying she'd just had word from Santa himself that he was worried about two little boys who weren't yet asleep. He couldn't possibly make a stop if they weren't tucked into their beds. The twins were off like a shot, with their father chasing after them to the back door. They were one of several families sleeping in the dorm rooms in the stables; the rest of the guests were spread across the house and cottages further afield. There was room enough for everyone.

"Good night, Granny," Max said, once the last guest had traipsed off to bed, completely exhausted. He gave the woman a hug. Kensy did too.

"Good night, my darlings," Cordelia said, sighing contentedly. "See you in the morning."

The twins walked to the door, surprised to see the entire buffet table had been cleared and the room was absolutely pristine again. They hadn't even noticed anyone packing up.

"That was incredible," Max said.

"It sure was. Granny's amazing," Kensy fizzed. Her cheeks were red and she had long ago ditched her Christmas sweater after working up a sweat on the dance floor. "And I don't care if you agree with me or not – Uncle Rupert is bags of fun."

Max was about to say something when he stopped dead and stared at his watch, which was vibrating wildly. It was fortunate he never took off the timepiece because Kensy was always misplacing hers. After almost losing it for good earlier in the day, she'd left it on her bedside table this evening.

"Hurry up, slowpoke, I want to get to bed before –" Kensy's eyes lit up as she realized what had captured his attention. "I bet Fitz has found them and they're on their way home! I knew he would!"

"We need to write this down," Max said, beginning to run. "Come on, the library's closest."

The pair scampered across the entrance foyer and along the hallway. Fortunately, the entire place was empty. Max and Kensy burst into the room and raced to the writing desk, where a lone brass lamp shone a dull glow. Max pulled open the drawer, snatched up a pencil and notepad then waited for the series of judders to begin again. He scribbled the Morse code dashes and dots, checking twice that he'd recorded it correctly.

"Well, what does it say?" Kensy whispered, peering over his shoulder.

Max tore the paper from the pad and held it up:

Happy Christmas, darlings. We love you.
Ciao for now. Mum and Dad.

Kensy turned to her brother and hugged him tightly. "But why can't they come home?" She brushed at the tears rolling down her cheeks.

A light snapped on in the far corner of the room, startling them both. Kensy's breath caught in her throat as she and Max spun around. She quickly wiped her eyes. Sitting in the armchair, with a copy of the *Beacon* spread across his lap, was their uncle.

Rupert folded the newspaper and grinned at the twins. "Good news?" he asked. "I mean, after what happened at the racetrack, it would be nice to have a positive spin on the day — pardon the pun."

Max shifted uncomfortably. "Um, we just wanted to write Granny a thank-you note." He tucked the piece of paper with the decoded message into his back pocket.

"Really?" Rupert cocked his head to one side. "My hearing must be playing up. I could have sworn I heard you say –"

A clock on the mantelpiece chimed the half hour.

"Oh goodness, is that the time?" Kensy yawned loudly and stretched her arms above her head while Max stood frozen to the spot beside her. "Wow, all that dancing must've taken it out of me. Uncle Rupert, you really know how to party. I might even need an ice pack after all those backflips. Well, less talking and more doing, as they say. We'd better get to bed or Santa will whiz right overhead. Come on, Max," she said, tugging on her brother's sleeve. "Good night!"

The twins were both conscious of Rupert's unwavering gaze.

"Sleep tight, kids," he said, taking up his newspaper. "Close the door on your way out."

Kensy pulled it shut behind them and looked at her brother. Without a word passing between them, they broke into a run and wound their way upstairs, not stopping to catch their breaths until they'd reached Max's bedroom door.

"Do you think he heard what we said?" Max panted. He hoped not. There was still something about Uncle Rupert that didn't sit easily with him despite his sister's enthusiasm.

Kensy shook her head. "Who knows? And what does it matter if he did? I wish we could tell Granny."

"Well, we can't," Max said.

Meanwhile, downstairs in the library, Rupert Spencer picked up a pencil and colored in the notepad with the deftest of touches. His eyebrows jumped up in surprise when he held it under the desk lamp. "So you're alive, after all, big brother," he muttered, and sat down, deep in thought.

CHAPTER 12

⁊∩◻ ∪∪< ∨∩∪ ⼕◻<<

The boy climbed out the window and onto the red tiled roof. The twinkling lights of the giant Christmas tree in the piazza shone from below, illuminating his fine features. He could see tourists swarming with their cameras. In the furthest corner, protestors kept vigil with their placards, warming themselves by the firelight of their makeshift furnaces while the *carabinieri* watched on. He had been annoyed to see a picture of himself with his mother on the front page of one of the newspapers just that morning. If the reports were true, his mother was fast becoming the most despised person in the country. The tree, with its million euros' worth of crystal decorations, was the most magnificent Rome had ever seen – and was now the cause of even greater civil unrest.

Nico adjusted the daypack on his back, then took a deep breath and ran, his feet featherlight across the rooftop. All those months of training with the parkour team were about to pay off and soon he would be celebrating Christmas with his grandfather, whether his mother approved or not. Why should she care, anyway? She had her new husband and the job she'd always wanted.

"Stop!"

Nico froze. He could see a guard in the piazza pointing up at him. Some of the tourists had turned to look too. He couldn't go back now. He wouldn't. Nico spun around. He needed a run-up or there was no way he would make it to the other side. It comforted him to know that only Fabrizio was fit enough to follow him.

Nico filled his lungs and began to sprint just as the door to the rooftop flew open. He charged toward the edge of the roof and, with his arms spinning like a windmill, leapt into the abyss. He was flying through the air when, with a stab of dread, he realized he'd miscalculated.

Nico slammed into the stone wall but managed to grab hold of an iron railing. As his body swung like a pendulum, Nico resisted the urge to look down. With a grunt, he hauled himself over the balcony railing, then somersaulted up onto the roof. He lay there for a second, his heart thumping in his chest. That had been much too close for comfort.

Over the din of car horns and traffic, Fabrizio called out his name. Nico propped up on his elbows, laughing at the sight of the man shaking his fist. "*Codardo!*" Nico shouted.

With a wave goodbye, the boy jumped to his feet and fled across the rooftops of Rome. It wouldn't be long until they raised the alert. He could already hear the wail of sirens.

Nico felt as if his chest was about to

explode as he leapt from building to building. He was making good progress, when a searchlight forced him to reassess his route. The helicopters had taken to the air faster than he'd anticipated. He would soon have to drop down into the shadows of the street, which was much more time-consuming. Nico came to another break in the rooflines and launched into the air. But as he landed, the tiles disintegrated like chalk beneath his feet. He could feel himself falling down, down, down and there was nothing he could do to stop it. He hit the floor below with a sickening thud.

* * *

"*Mamma mia!*" the woman exclaimed as she heard the ruckus from above. She charged up the narrow staircase to the top of the vast town house. "Giovanni, come quickly!" she screeched.

There was a snort and grumbling from the bedroom below. "What is it?" he called, unhappy to have been woken.

"Just get up here!" she ordered. "Now!"

Giovanni did as he was bid and shuffled into the room, rubbing his eyes. The disused space with its peeling paint was filled with cast-off furniture piled high around the walls and a narrow single bed in the corner. Lying in the middle of the floor, which was peppered with shards of broken tiles, was a child. Giovanni peered up at the gaping hole in the roof. "Since when do young boys fall from the sky?"

The woman knelt over the lad. A trickle of blood ran down the child's temple, but he had a strong pulse and was breathing. She looked up at the man. "Perhaps he is a gift from God."

The man gazed at the boy's face. There was something familiar about it. He blinked again, then sped away only to return clutching a newspaper. "Do you know who this is?" he said, thrusting it into the woman's hands.

She stared at the front page then at the boy, before stepping back with her hand on her heart. "The Lord works in mysterious ways," she said, clasping her hands together. "Quickly, Giovanni, get up there and fix those tiles!"

CHAPTER 13

⬜◻◻◹◲⬡

Max rubbed his sleepy eyes and pushed himself up against the pillows. It took him a few seconds to remember where he was and that it was Christmas Day – the first he'd ever spent apart from his parents. Although he'd always cherish last night's celebrations, Max would have given anything for his mum to be sitting on the edge of the bed and his dad goofing around in the background. Just to hear their voices would be the best gift ever.

With a sigh, Max slipped out of bed and walked to the window. He pulled back the heavy drapes as Kensy barreled through the door in her dressing gown and slippers, carrying a large parcel. She dumped it onto the bed and crash tackled him with a boisterous hug. "Happy Christmas, little brother."

Max grinned. "Happy Christmas, big sister by thirty minutes," he said, smoothing his hair.

Kensy took a deep breath and stepped back, wiping her eyes. "Before you say anything, I'm not crying, okay? We know Mum and Dad are fine – fine enough to keep in contact, anyway – and I've been thinking about their message. They said '*ciao*.' Doesn't that mean 'bye' in Italian? Do you think they were hinting to their location? They could be in Italy, Max."

He'd had the exact same thought, though he hadn't planned on sharing it with his sister, knowing how prone she was to being hasty. "It would certainly be ironic if they were," Max conceded, "with us traveling to Rome tomorrow on the school history tour."

"We should get word to Fitz!" Kensy exclaimed.

"Steady on, Kens," Max cautioned. "We don't know for certain that's where they are – we're only guessing." He fetched a beautifully wrapped gift from the desk and handed it to her. The paper was made from a white pearlescent stock and bordered by prancing reindeer with glittery red noses and flanks flecked with gold leaf. Song had helped the boy to source it from the Burlington Arcade, the man's favorite stationery shop in London.

Beaming, Kensy grabbed the parcel with both hands. She held it to her ear and shook it vigorously, eliciting a grimace from her brother. "Wait, I got you something too," she said, and scooped up Max's gift from where she'd abandoned it on the bed. "Sorry, I'm not very good at wrapping."

The Santa-patterned paper was crumpled and torn in places where the girl had clearly encountered difficulty. Kensy appeared to have used several rolls of tape and undertaken the task wearing oven mitts. While she wouldn't win any prizes for presentation, Max appreciated the effort.

Kensy tore the paper off her present and was surprised to find another box to open. Max, meanwhile, took his time hunting for the end of a piece of tape. Kensy lifted the lid and pulled out a gilded birdcage with two miniature robins inside it. One was sitting on a swing and the other was on the floor. Kensy held it up and examined it closely, turning the object in her hands until she spied the mechanism.

"Oh, Max, it's an automaton! It's like Granny's elephant downstairs but tiny." She wound the key and gasped as the birds began to flitter and chirp. The one on the floor flew up and around the cage while the other did loops on the swing.

The boy grinned at her. Max knew she would be itching to pull it apart to see how it all worked. "Promise me you'll leave it in one piece for today at least."

Kensy wrinkled her nose. "Only if you insist. You know I'll put it back exactly as it was – if not better."

Max nodded and finished opening his present. He was awestruck when he realized what it was. "How on earth did you manage to get this?" he asked her.

"Fitz and Song helped me. We found it in an antiques shop on Portobello Road," Kensy said proudly. "It's way better than the bag of rocks you collected for me when I was six, that's for sure."

"Really?" Max laughed at the memory, and it felt good to remember happier times. "I thought you loved them. Dad said they were magic."

"Magic my eye." Kensy shook her head. "I believed anything back then."

"You should consider that payback for the handle you unscrewed from our bedroom door and tried to convince me I could use as a portal to another world the Christmas before." Max placed his gift onto his lap and began tapping away on his very own enigma machine. It was a contraption invented by a German engineer, Dr. Arthur Scherbius, at the end of World War I. Said to be the most sophisticated cipher machine ever developed, it looked much like a typewriter but used a series of rotors and electrical currents to randomly assign a code.

During World War II, a clever Englishman called Alan Turing managed to crack the German's cipher. It has been said that Turing's work shortened the war by two years and probably saved over fourteen million lives.

Kensy returned the automaton to its box and walked over to the window. "Have you seen the garden yet? Autumn said it would snow. It's beautiful . . . Mum and Dad would love it here."

In the early-morning light, the estate sparkled. The lollipop trees along the top of the wall closest to the house looked as if they'd been dusted with icing sugar, and the Atlas fountain was frozen solid. Autumn had only told Kensy the week before that the fountain was another one of the estate's treasures, with a strong room beneath it containing yet more secrets to be discovered. Apparently, none of the junior agents had ever been inside – it required top-level security clearance – so they weren't even absolutely sure it existed. Kensy couldn't wait to investigate further.

A line of taxis could be seen heading for

the main gates. Kensy frowned, not recalling anything in the itinerary about off-site activities this morning. She hoped they hadn't missed an important instruction. While it wouldn't have been unusual for her, it would be highly out of character for Max. She didn't have to wait long to find out as her train of thought was interrupted by a knock on the door.

"Good morning, children, and a very merry Christmas to you," Song said, entering the room with a bow. Unlike the twins, who were still in their pajamas, Song was dressed in his customary tuxedo. Over the past few days, the butler had donned a variety of outfits ranging from casual clothes to last night's ugly sweater. It seemed a bit glum now that he was back in full work mode – especially today.

"Happy Christmas to you too, Song," Max said.

"Where's everyone going?" Kensy asked, pointing out the window.

"All will be revealed in due course. Your grandmother wishes to see you in her suite," Song replied. "I cannot tell you any more, Miss

Kensington, no matter how hard you try to get it out of me. Not even if you bought me the complete collection of Johnny Cash for my Christmas present."

Kensy giggled. "As if that would ever happen."

Max shrugged on his dressing gown and slippers and together the children followed Song to their grandmother's suite. The butler gently tapped on the door and, after a generous pause, ushered the children inside, where they found Cordelia on the phone. She mouthed her apologies and gestured for them to make themselves comfortable. Max noticed that she was also still in her pajamas, which he found oddly comforting.

"Thank you, Gabriel, and a very happy Christmas to you and the family," she said warmly. "Oh, and please tell Catherine I'm looking forward to seeing her at the fundraiser next week. Goodbye, dear." Cordelia put down the phone and sat back with a sigh. "Sorry, darlings. The prime minister doesn't like to be ignored."

Kensy and Max smiled wryly at one

another. Of course their grandmother would be exchanging Christmas greetings with the prime minister of England. Didn't everyone? Max had been gobsmacked to read some of the cards that had arrived from dignitaries around the world. Among them had been a beautiful hamper sealed with the royal warrant, which had been sent directly from Her Majesty. Cordelia held out her arms and the twins rushed into them.

"Where's everyone off to?" Kensy asked. She couldn't help but feel she was missing out on the fun.

"A major mission went live late last night," Cordelia said, stifling a yawn. "It appears that those who wish to do the world harm do not have any consideration for public holidays or celebrations. It's to be expected, I suppose. Quite a few of our guests left straight after the party and everyone else is setting off now."

Kensy's chest tightened. "Does it have anything to do with Mum and Dad?"

Cordelia shook her head. "A world leader is in peril, along with several hundred thousand civilians should our people fail."

Kensy felt a pang of relief followed by a stab of guilt. She was glad her parents weren't involved, but so many other people's loved ones were. All of a sudden it didn't feel much like Christmas.

"Has everyone gone?" Max asked, already knowing what the answer would be.

Cordelia nodded and touched his chin. "I'm afraid you're stuck with me and the household staff," she said with a wink. "The operation is all hands on deck for now. Your friends and teachers will, however, be on your three o'clock flight to Rome tomorrow."

"Why couldn't we go on the mission? We're ready," Kensy huffed. She immediately remembered who she was speaking to and looked down at her slippers, chastened. Although Cordelia was their grandmother, she was also the head of Pharos and important enough to receive hampers from the queen. It wouldn't do her cause any favors to behave like a spoiled child – even Kensy knew that. It was just so frustrating to be mollycoddled all the time. She was burning to be able to help.

"Oh, darling, we don't ever use the children on assignments unless we absolutely have to," Cordelia said.

Kensy bit her lip. "So, we're not up to scratch?"

"I didn't say that at all." Her grandmother raised an eyebrow. "You are both doing incredibly well, but, believe me, fieldwork is not for the fainthearted and you have years of excitement ahead of you. Besides, I wish I was going to Rome with Mr. Reffell – the man's a walking history book. You'll have a wonderful time."

"Granny's right," Max said. "We've only just started training. What if we messed up? We could endanger a lot more people than ourselves."

Kensy rolled her eyes.

"Anyway, let's not sit around and mope," Cordelia said, springing to her feet. "I think there might be something special for both of you under that tree over there and after lunch we're going to deliver gifts to all of the children who live on the estate – and take dinner for their families too. We can't let Mrs. Thornthwaite's feast go to waste." Cordelia's phone rang. "But I think there's someone who'd like to wish you both a happy Christmas first." She lifted the device so the children could see the caller.

"Fitz!" the twins gasped. Kensy pushed in front of her brother, who had to manhandle her to the side so Fitz could see them both.

He was clearly holding the phone in one hand away from his face – although every now and then he forgot and they had an up-close image of the inside of his (very clean) nose. "Hi, kids, are you having a good morning?"

Max took the phone from Cordelia and held it out in front of him.

"Where are you?" Kensy asked. "Have you found –" She stopped and checked herself. "I mean, happy Christmas."

The children chatted to Fitz for several minutes, regaling him with all the stories from the night before. He said he'd heard about their accident too and was very proud of the way they'd handled themselves. When their grandmother left the room to check on breakfast, they told him about their latest message from their parents.

"Have you found anything?" Max asked. His eyes searched the screen for clues as to the man's whereabouts, but all he had to work with was the image of Fitz standing in front of a window covered by a sheer curtain.

Fitz shook his head. The twins told him about everyone leaving and what the day had in store. Max also thanked him for helping Kensy find the best present ever. Just as they were saying their goodbyes, the curtain behind Fitz flapped in the breeze and the sun lit up the view. The children could see a silhouette of rooftops and a large dome.

"You have a great time in Rome," Fitz said with a smile. "And I'll see you soon. I promise."

Once the call had ended, Max looked at Kensy, a glimmer of hope in his blue eyes. "Perhaps sooner than we think."

CHAPTER 14

ΛΓΕΕΓ˩˥

Vittoria Vitale stared daggers at the uniformed man before her. "Are you telling me there is no sign of my son?" she said through gritted teeth.

The fellow shifted awkwardly under her gaze. "I am sorry, Prime Minister. It is as if the boy has fallen off the face of the earth. My men and I have looked everywhere. We have searched the railway and bus stations, and an entire team is reviewing all of the closed-circuit television footage within the city limits. We have also knocked on every door of every household and business for miles. I am afraid that, if he has not returned by this evening, we must alert the media and appeal to the public for their help."

"The public help *me*?" Vittoria scoffed, fiddling with the pear-shaped diamond on her ring finger. "They hate me enough as it is – and will revel in my failure as a mother."

"Mia cara." Her husband hurried to her side. Although in his late forties, the man was striking with thick dark hair, olive skin and eyes like pools of black ink. "If anyone is to blame, it is me," he said, wrapping his arms around her. "I should have paid more attention to the boy."

But how? Vittoria knew nothing would have appeased her son, who only wanted to return to their hometown to be with his grandfather. Ever since they had moved to Rome, he had been near impossible, arguing with her and Lorenzo constantly. It was lucky her husband had the patience of a saint. In truth, she had on more than one occasion investigated boarding schools in Switzerland and England. Life was complicated enough trying to run the country without familial drama adding to her load. But now that her worst nightmare had been realized, the only thing she wished for was to be reunited with her little boy.

* * *

Nico rubbed his pounding head and squinted into the darkness as a mustiness enveloped him. The last thing he could remember was running across the rooftops, away from that lout Fabrizio.

The aroma of garlic and herbs hung in the air, making his stomach grumble. Nico sat up gingerly. "Hello?" he called. "Is anyone there?"

Outside, the floorboards squeaked. Someone was coming. The handle turned and the door creaked open to reveal a silhouetted figure.

"H-Hello, could you tell me where I am? I seem to have forgotten . . ." Nico trailed off as a man wearing a black balaclava deposited a tray of food by the door.

"*Buon Natale*," the man said over his shoulder then left.

Nico heard a key turn in the lock and, ignoring his aching limbs, ran to the door. "Please come back! I need to go home," he yelled, banging his fists against the door. "Let me out! Please!"

The boy shouted for what felt like an eternity before he gave up and sat down on the bare floorboards. Through the haze in his head, he remembered. It was Christmas Day, but he had a horrible feeling that there would be no celebrations here.

CHAPTER 15

⬚ԱΛᴑ

Max stared out the window as the plane descended through a patch of clouds into Leonardo da Vinci–Fiumicino Airport, some sixteen miles from the center of Rome. It was strange to think that only a couple of days ago they were in full training mode at Alexandria and now they were back to being regular kids on a school trip, with not a word of the past week to be uttered aloud. Max wondered how the others never slipped up, but supposed that the longer one led a double life, the easier it might become to lie. He hoped he wouldn't make any mistakes. Granted, it was more likely that Kensy would blurt out something. Indeed, several rows in front, his sister had tried everything she could to extract information about the Christmas mission from Autumn. Each time, Autumn managed to steer the conversation in a different direction. That girl was effortlessly polite and a seasoned professional.

In no time flat, the children, along with Mrs. Vanden Boom, Mr. Frizzle, Miss Ziegler and Mr. Reffell, had disembarked, cleared immigration and boarded a minibus. Mr. Reffell sat at the front, commentating their journey into the city and pointing out various landmarks. It was a noisy ride among the beeping horns as cars and scooters darted in and out of the traffic. Their driver, Franco, cheerfully bore the brunt of much abuse, to the children's great amusement – particularly among those who knew an Italian swear word or two.

"Are we going to the Colosseum this afternoon, sir?" Alfie called out.

"If you care to consult your itinerary, you'll see that we have a half-day tour there tomorrow." The man raised his eyebrows. "It's going to be amazing – just wait until you see what I have planned."

Romilly Vanden Boom blanched. A statement like that from Monty set her teeth on edge – heaven knew what the man had up his sleeve.

"When are we going to the Vatican?" Lola asked. "I want a blessing from the pope."

Autumn looked at Kensy and whispered, "She needs more than a blessing."

Kensy snorted with laughter, garnering a glare from the girl.

Monty Reffell sighed audibly. "Might I suggest that you all have a read of the detailed pages that were included in the folder that I gave out to each and every one of you before we boarded the plane?"

"But I left mine in my seat pocket," moaned Graham Churchill. He was always forgetting things and quite literally scratching his head.

"Good heavens, man, we've only been here a minute. How could you have lost something

162

already?" Monty frowned. "It's just as well I made extras, although I'm not giving you another one until tomorrow. You can share with someone else for now. Actually, share with Lola – she doesn't seem to know what's going on either. I'm sure you two will love being buddies for the afternoon."

Lola Lemmler looked as if she might throw up. "But Graham's *gross*! I'm not sharing with him. *Misha's* my buddy."

Eyes widened around the bus and there was a flurry of whispers.

"Lola, you will apologize to Graham at once and you *will* be his buddy for the rest of the day," Monty declared.

"It's okay, sir. I'd rather not. Lola's a nasty cow," Graham retorted, to the muffled guffaws of his classmates.

Lola leapt up, almost strangling herself with the seat belt in the process. She wrestled free, then marched over to the lad, who was sitting across the aisle two rows back. "What did you say?" she demanded. Although small in stature, Lola possessed an intimidating air and had been known to reduce senior students and even teachers to tears.

"You heard me," the boy said, jutting out his chin. "Unless those dainty ears of yours are full of wax."

Mr. Reffell yawned theatrically. "Lola, sit down before I instruct the driver to turn around and deposit you back at the airport."

"But he called me a cow." The girl's long lashes fluttered as her eyes filled with tears.

The man sighed again. "And you said he was gross."

"So? He *is*," Lola sulked. "Everyone knows he's got nits!"

At the mention of the critters, half the bus scratched their heads. Kensy and Max hated to indulge the upstart, but they couldn't help themselves and began itching their scalps too. Mr. Reffell was no exception, much to his own annoyance.

"Right," Romilly Vanden Boom barked, standing up from her seat in the middle of the bus. "You will *both* apologize or I'll gladly send you *both* home. This is hardly an auspicious start to what should be a wonderful week." The woman's voice reverberated through the bus, causing even the driver to shiver in fear.

"But my parents are here in Italy," Lola grouched under her breath.

Misha looked over at the girl. This was news to her. Lola hadn't mentioned a thing about it before and she was usually quite the open book.

"Well, in that case," Mrs. Vanden Boom replied, arching an eyebrow, "I'd imagine they'd be very happy to collect you right away."

Lola gulped, knowing that wouldn't be the case at all. Her father had spent Christmas away and her mother had flown out yesterday evening to join him. She had been left at home with her nonna, who had accompanied her to the airport.

Lottie Ziegler and Elliot Frizzle, who were sitting at the back of the bus, snickered like schoolchildren. Truth be told, neither of them would have minded the girl being sent home. Misha had her work cut out for her, that was for sure, and the girl pulled it off with poise.

At times it was difficult to discern where her undercover persona ended and the real Misha began, which earned her the respect of her teachers as well as her Pharos peers.

"She'd do it, you know," Carlos whispered to Max. "Mrs. V.B. would send them home in a heartbeat. She takes no prisoners."

Graham caved first. "Sorry, Lola, I didn't mean to call you a cow. You're probably not."

Everyone turned and stared in Lola's direction to see what she'd do next. Given no one on the bus could remember her ever apologizing for anything, it must have been killing her.

Lola flicked her ponytail over her shoulder and inspected her painted fingernails. She glanced at Misha, who flashed a sympathetic smile. Lola took a deep, shaky breath. "Sorry, Graham," she said in a tiny voice.

Romilly looked at Monty, who shrugged. "Well, I suppose that will do," she said. "Now, I don't want to hear another bad word from either of you for the rest of the trip or, mark my words, I will make good on my promise."

"Do you think they'll still have to be buddies?" Max asked Carlos.

The boy grinned. "Definitely. The teachers will take great pleasure in that. Might be some fireworks later."

Lola sat back down with a thud and folded her arms while Graham scratched his head. The bus wound its way through the narrow streets into the heart of the city. They passed beautiful churches and ancient ruins alongside modern supermarkets and fast-food outlets that seemed completely at odds with the patina of a civilization thousands of years old, yet at the same time it made perfect sense. There was traffic and people everywhere and lots of police on scooters and on horseback.

When their bus pulled up outside a hotel, Monty Refell stood up and clapped his hands to get the children's attention. He waved an arm at the enormous fountain directly opposite them. "That's the –"

"Trevi Fountain!" Inez squealed, jiggling up and down in her seat. Ever since she'd visited the Palace of Versailles in France, the girl had developed a fascination with baroque architecture and prided herself on being able to identify buildings and structures in that style.

Mr. Reffell was delighted by her enthusiasm. "Yes, you're absolutely right, Inez. It's a beauty, isn't it?" he said wistfully. "We'll take a proper look once we're settled in. Our first activity will be a walk to acquaint ourselves with the area. Now, here's a fun fact. Did you know that the ancient Romans actually invented concrete and, after the fall of the Roman Empire, the formula was lost for over a thousand years? Fascinating stuff."

The children alighted from the bus and several of them assisted the driver in unloading the luggage. Mr. Reffell went ahead to organize the rooms and keys.

"Frizzle!" Franco called, holding up an old-fashioned suitcase.

"It's pronounced Friz-*zel*." Elliot sighed, grabbing his bag. He really had to do something about changing that spelling.

Kensy and Autumn turned circles, taking it all in. In addition to the hotel opposite the fountain, the structure was surrounded by an assortment of buildings, many of them old and painted in traditional terra-cotta red with shutters and ornate plasterwork, as well as a wedding cake-like church called Santi Vincenzo e Anastasio a Trevi further along on the corner. There were open-air shops and hawkers peddling their wares to the tourists.

Max spotted a poster on the wall beside the hotel entrance. It was the front page of a newspaper with a photograph of a boy taking up most of the real estate. "Hey, Carlos, check this out," he said, walking over to have a closer look. The masthead read "*Scomparso.*"

"Do you know what it says?" Carlos asked. "Italian isn't my strong suit, but we could ask Dante to interpret."

Kensy and Autumn had wandered over to see what the boys were looking at. Max scanned the page and, while his own Italian was far from perfect, he got the gist of the article. "The prime minister's son is missing. It says that he ran away on Christmas Eve and hasn't been seen since."

"That's terrible," Autumn said, as they were joined by Harper and Dante. "How old is he?"

"Twelve, and they say it's as if he vanished into a puff of smoke," Kensy added.

Harper gasped. "His parents must be beside themselves."

"He might be a brat," Dante said, scanning the article to see if there was any hint of the boy's personality.

"Even still, I imagine his parents would be awfully upset," Harper replied.

"Maybe that explains why there are so many *poliziotti* and *carabinieri* on the streets," Max mused. "Perhaps they're looking for him."

Dante shook his head. "No, they're always around. My dad jokes that there are more police per person in Rome than anywhere else on the planet and yet thousands of tourists are pickpocketed each year."

Mr. Reffell stood at the hotel entrance and called to the children.

Autumn nudged Kensy and pointed to the far side of the fountain. "Now, that looks like a scene from a movie."

A nun dressed in a traditional habit with a wimple on her head was leading a trail of a dozen children, ranging from five to twelve years of age, across the piazza. They were modestly dressed with neat hair and polished shoes. Kensy couldn't help noticing the woman had a very large nose and a stoop. Two stern-faced men, with shirts buttoned all the way to the top, flanked either side of the line and another followed up at the rear. They were heading toward the church.

"They are orphans," Franco told the group. "That is Sister Maria Regina, bless her soul. She is a saint – not technically, but she will surely be one day. She is a kind woman with a big heart and that is her orphanage there."

Kensy's eyes settled on a dark-haired boy with long hair that skimmed the tops of his eyes. When he looked up, she smiled and waved. He raised his hand to wave back, but the man beside him said something that caused the boy's gaze to drop to the ground. Kensy watched him walk away, his head bowed, and noticed a mark behind his ear – it almost looked like a tattoo. How could that be for a boy his age? Kensy wondered what the man had said to him. Maybe the children weren't supposed to be friendly to strangers. But she was just a girl herself and hardly a threat to the lad.

"Poor kid," Kensy mumbled as she followed her friends inside.

CHAPTER 16

THE PICKPOCKET

The children were soon settled into the hotel, having taken over the entire establishment. There were sixteen students in total – eight girls and eight boys. Eleven of them were Pharos agents-in-training while the remaining five were regular kids. Kensy was sharing with Autumn in a twin bedroom under the eaves. It was a charming space with ancient beams overhead and decorative Ionic columns on either side of the bathroom vanity. The girls were pleasantly surprised at how lovely it was.

Max was rooming with Carlos on the floor below, and next to them was Inez, sharing with a girl called Harriet, who had a crown of unruly chestnut curls and a quick temper. Alfie found himself bunking with Graham, but didn't mind in the least. Apart from the earlier episode on the bus, Graham was one of those people who just rolled with the punches. There were another two lads – Liam and Winston – who were inseparable friends, and Misha was sharing with Lola.

Kensy couldn't help thinking how much harder it would be rooming with someone who wasn't part of the organization, and was all the more grateful for being paired with Autumn.

The children had been instructed to meet in the restaurant on the third floor, which overlooked the fountain. There they would have a light snack before their first excursion. On offer were generous plates of antipasto, filled with salami, cheese, olives and artichoke hearts. When Mrs. Vanden Boom enquired after some bread and grissini to accompany the platters, the young waitress eyed her warily.

"Is there a problem?" Romilly asked. In her experience, the Italians loved to fill up their guests with bread. There was many a time she'd been full before the first course had arrived.

The waitress wiped her hands on her apron. "I'm sorry, *signora*, it is just that my boss has told me to be sparing with the bread. There is a wheat shortage and the prices have become astronauts." She smiled apologetically. "I will see what I can do."

Romilly thanked the girl and resisted the urge to tell her she had meant to say "astronomical." She had recently read something in the newspaper at home about the pending crisis but hadn't realized it had reached such dire straits.

The children plowed their way through the snacks while Mr. Reffell made sure that everyone was equipped with a small foldout map of the vicinity. In the unlikely event that anyone became separated from the group, they would be able to find their way back to the hotel. Monty then allocated a staff member to each group of four students. Mr. Frizzle was to watch over Kensy, Autumn, Max and Carlos, while Mrs. Vanden Boom had volunteered to take care of Misha, Lola, Alfie and Graham. None of that foursome seemed terribly happy about the fact, but Romilly was quietly looking forward to it. She was hoping there might be an opportunity to make the children hold hands at some stage – for safety reasons, of course. It brought a grin to her lips just thinking about how Lola would react to being within five feet of poor old Graham.

"Now, you must take extra care when crossing the roads – and keep your eyes peeled when walking along the sidewalks," Monty warned. "Drivers here tend to have a blatant disregard for the road rules." He held aloft a small red flag with a picture of Julius Caesar's face on it. "If you are ever in doubt, look for this."

"That's not very original, sir," Dante piped up. "Don't you think there might be other tour groups with the same thing?"

The man sighed. "What would you suggest then, Moretti?"

"Maybe a skull and crossbones," the boy said, garnering snorts of laughter.

Monty Reffell rolled his eyes. "Perhaps we'll save that for a trip to the Caribbean."

"Sir, we're wearing uniforms," Harper pointed out. "That should keep us together."

"Unfortunately," Lola grumbled.

By the time the group bundled out onto the street, the crowd in front of the Trevi Fountain had swelled. The throng was twenty people deep, meaning there was little chance of getting close to the monument for some time. The *poliziotti* were busy trying to keep the tourists moving. Mr. Reffell quickly decided they would visit later in the evening, when the swarm should have dissipated. Nevertheless, it was a dazzling afternoon – fifty-five degrees with a bright azure sky. Compared with much of Europe, Rome was known to have reasonably mild winters.

"Why are people throwing coins over their shoulders into the water?" Winston asked.

"It's supposed to be good luck and means that you'll come back to Rome again one day,"

Mr. Frizzle explained. "In ancient times, Romans threw in a coin to please the water gods and to ensure a safe journey. They also say that, if you throw two coins, you'll find love, and if you throw three, you will be married."

"Maybe I should try that," Lottie Ziegler muttered under her breath. "Because nothing seems to have worked so far."

Autumn was secretly thinking the same thing. She glanced at Max, who was walking up ahead of them. Kensy didn't miss it and nudged her friend in the ribs. Mr. Reffell led the children out of the crowded area and past the orphanage. The narrow, winding streets revealed charming piazzas, where people sat drinking coffee while watching the world go by.

Monty had plotted a course designed to introduce the children to an array of Roman delights and to help them get a feel for the city. He could still remember the first time he'd visited when he was a young man in his second year at university. That trip had spurred a lifelong love affair not just with Rome but with all things Italian, including his beautiful wife. But that seemed a million years ago. Just being here made him smile – in spite of the tragedy that had taken her life.

It wasn't long before the narrow streets gave way to a much larger market square complete with a tall column in the center – yet another monument to someone of importance in the Roman empire.

Kensy's eyes were everywhere as she took in the milieu. She loved people watching and the elegant Italians were impeccably dressed in designer clothing, strolling arm in arm. She marveled at the women in towering heels negotiating the uneven cobblestones as if they were walking on the smoothest of roadways, while the tourists were obvious in their jeans and sneakers and daypacks. Another school group, wearing black-and-white uniforms, flocked around a small rotunda that was selling drinks and souvenirs on the far side of the piazza.

When they had finally reached their first destination, Monty Reffell thrust his flag in the air and beckoned the children to gather around as he launched into a rather lengthy explanation of the origins of the Spanish Steps.

"Can we sit down, sir?" Sachin asked. Although they had only been walking for twenty minutes, at times it had felt as though they were ocean swimmers pushing against a crushing swell.

"Oh yes, of course," Mr. Reffell said. "Find a spot."

Romilly was glad the lad had asked as she was feeling a tad weary herself. The group spread out across a couple of rows a few flights up. Fortunately, the steps were so wide there was still plenty of room for people to use them as they were originally intended.

Mr. Reffell started up again, but this time he was interrupted by Mr. Frizzle, the children's art teacher.

"Did you know that, because of their unique design, the steps have always attracted artists who in turn enticed beautiful young women keen to try their hands as models, which henceforth brought out wealthy young men eager to pursue them. The Spanish Steps have been a popular gathering place in Rome for centuries. I mean, even now I can see at least four easels perched up there."

"Fascinating, Mr. Frizzle," Monty Reffell said, clearly wanting the stage back again. "But I have a few more *historical* facts that the children will be keen to hear and I hope they're paying attention because we might have a little pop quiz tonight over dinner."

Lottie Ziegler was a million miles away. It had been a busy week and she was still on call for code-breaking duties should she be needed. Lottie prided herself on her loyalty to Pharos and her track record of undertaking each assignment without a note of complaint, but there was a tiny part of her that wished she'd been able to go along with the active agents on this most recent mission. Although she loved teaching math and mentoring the junior agents-in-training, every now and then she yearned to be in the field.

Kensy was similarly distracted. A boy pulling a cart full of blocks had caught her eye. She wondered if they might have been a present from Santa and was remembering her own enormous collection when a woman standing in a doorway began shouting. A young man wearing a flat cap and waistcoat over a white shirt was the target of her anger. She grabbed him by the ear and marched him inside. Kensy understood enough to ascertain that the woman was his mother and he was supposed to be at home helping with chores but had been off playing cards with his ne'er-do-well mates.

The pair went inside and Kensy's gaze fell upon a boy in a navy puffer jacket and jeans. He looked to be on his own and was walking closely behind a man in a suit with a newspaper tucked under his arm. She watched him brush against the fellow and his hand disappear into a pocket that wasn't his own.

"Look!" Autumn pointed at a bridal party that was strolling toward them, but Kensy couldn't take her eyes off the boy.

A second later, the lad vanished into the throng and she was sure he had taken the man's wallet along with him.

"Hey!" Kensy stood up and leapt two steps at a time down to the piazza. She dodged the crowds and raced as quickly as she could toward the man. "*Scusi, signore!*" she shouted, not daring to look away in case she lost him. Fortunately, he stopped outside the door of a coffeehouse.

"*Signore*, I think you've been robbed," she panted. When he regarded her quizzically, Kensy thought for a moment, trying to recall the right word. *"Derubato?"*

The man's eyes widened and he immediately reached into his back pocket. She was stunned when he pulled out his wallet and shook his head. He even opened it up to make sure that everything was still there.

Kensy swallowed hard, the heat rising to her cheeks. "*Mi scusi*," she said, turning back toward the street. She could have sworn she saw the young boy reach into the fellow's pocket. Now she just felt silly and was bound to be in a heap of trouble.

"Kensington Grey, what on earth do you think you're doing?" Romilly Vanden Boom demanded as she reached the girl.

"I thought I saw a pickpocket," Kensy replied. The fact that she had completely misread the situation didn't bode well for her upcoming evaluation. Kensy had recently learned that all Pharos agents-in-training received detailed reports on their progress every three months.

The woman arched a thick black eyebrow. "And did you?"

Kensy shook her head.

"Never mind," the woman said, to the girl's surprise. "One can't be too careful in Rome. Tourists are well-known targets for thieves."

"You're not angry?" Kensy asked.

Romilly Vanden Boom considered the girl. "Why would I be? A huge part of your life is about being on the lookout and protecting the public – even though they should never know it."

"But I got it wrong," Kensy said.

"Oh, my dear girl, you're going to get a lot more things wrong than that," the woman said with a smile. "Let's just hope that none of your mistakes put you in any real danger. Now, let's head back to the Spanish Steps and rescue the tourists who seem to think Mr. Reffell is some sort of official city guide. I fear he's turned into the troll from *Three Billy Goats Gruff* and isn't letting anyone pass until they can recite three facts for him."

Kensy walked along beside the teacher, but something made her look back. She was surprised to see the boy in the blue jacket standing with the man and even more shocked to see the lad pull a wallet from his pocket and hand it over. The fellow grinned widely and patted the lad's shoulder before the boy scampered off into the crowd. Kensy's mind was churning. No matter which way she looked at it, none of it made any sense at all.

CHAPTER 17

LUJCГOΛJ7ГUJ

Mr. Reffell guided the group along the Via del Babuino to the stunning Piazza del Popolo with its twin churches and ancient Egyptian obelisk. Surrounded by neoclassical buildings, the enormous square was practically empty compared with other parts of the city. A trail of senior citizens on Segways zipped past while three mounted policemen stood guard in the center of the open space. The children bounded about, taking loads of photographs and trying to spot the differences between the two adjacent Santa Maria churches, which, upon closer inspection, were not identical at all. Mr. Reffell pointed out numerous other landmarks, including the Villa Borghese gardens, which they would visit later in the week along with the Villa Medici on Pincian Hill.

As the obelisk cast long shadows from the afternoon sun and the temperature began to fall, several of the children were shivering and the decision was made to turn back for the hotel. Max walked along beside Carlos and Dante, who were talking excitedly about their upcoming visit to the Colosseum.

"Do you think we'll get to walk inside the hypogeum, where the gladiators and animals were held underground?" Carlos asked. "I read that it was two stories and there were thirty-six trapdoors that they could burst out of into the arena at any time. Imagine standing there and all of a sudden a lion jumps on you, or a gladiator. Which do you think would have been scarier?"

"Lion," Dante replied emphatically. "What about you, Max?"

But the boy's thoughts were elsewhere. Ever since they'd arrived in the city, he'd been thinking about his parents and wondering if that cryptic message on Christmas Eve had really meant anything. What were they looking for – or hiding from? And Max was almost certain the skyline they'd glimpsed while speaking to Fitz yesterday was of Rome, so it was entirely possible they were *all* here. Among the thousands of tourists, though, it didn't seem likely that he and Kensy would find them. Earlier, he'd spotted a bald, broad-shouldered man in the crowd and, for a fleeting moment, Max had thought it was Fitz. Then the man turned to reveal a thin moustache and coal-colored eyes. Max glanced over at his friends. "Sorry, what did you say?"

But Carlos and Dante had moved on and were talking about whether or not there might be ancient bloodstains in the arena. They were going to see if Mrs. Vanden Boom had a DNA kit with her.

The group took a different route this time, heading down the Via del Corso, past shops and restaurants, hotels and more monuments. Restauranteurs shouted from doorways, urging diners to choose their establishment. As they neared another piazza with yet another central memorial, this time celebrating the victories of Marcus Aurelius, the shouting intensified and the friendly tones grew harsh.

"Oh, good heavens," Mr. Reffell said. "The Italians do love a protest, don't they?"

Up ahead, an angry mob surrounded the stone column, chanting and holding aloft placards. There was a long line of armed *carabinieri* standing in front of an imposing building while a throng of photographers gathered as close as they dared to the giant front doors.

"What are they upset about, sir?" Inez asked.

"I gather they are protesting the price of wheat and the shortages of grain," the man said. "That's the Palazzo Chigi, where the Italian prime minister lives."

"And they're calling her a lying swine," Dante added.

"That's a bit insensitive considering her son is missing," Max said.

Several of the children looked at him blankly. "How do you know that?" Lola asked.

"There was the front page of a newspaper on the wall outside the hotel. It said he'd run away and was last seen on Christmas Eve," Kensy chimed in.

"The boy has been acting out since his mother remarried and she became prime minister," Lottie Ziegler added, noting that she'd read that in the paper too. The truth was, the information had come through from HQ that morning. After a quick assessment, Nico Vitale's disappearance had been downgraded from an international incident to a mere case of a flighty boy with a penchant for tantrums.

A soaring Christmas tree sparkled in the center of the palazzo, its crystal ornaments catching the light like millions of tiny stars. Suddenly, the crowd's chanting intensified as a black Mercedes Benz zoomed into the square and screeched to a halt outside the front doors.

A woman dressed head to toe in black walked out of the building, accompanied by a suave-looking man in a suit. Ignoring the hordes of photographers and journalists jostling for her attention, the prime minister hopped into the back of the car. Seconds later, it sped past the children, the photographers chasing after them, their flashbulbs like tiny explosions in the chilly evening air.

"So that was the prime minister," Kensy said. "I wouldn't fancy her job for all the money in the world."

Autumn shook her head. "I hope they find her son soon. She must be worried sick."

"I know that feeling," Kensy said as they turned left into a side street.

Autumn reached out and held her friend's hand, giving it a reassuring squeeze. At that moment Kensy's watch vibrated on her wrist. It emitted a long beep followed by three short staccato bursts. Instinctively, Kensy pulled away.

"I – I have to talk to Max," she said quickly, and pushed past the others to get to her brother, who was walking with his friends behind Mr. Reffell. She hadn't even reached him when she heard Max ask permission to run ahead to the hotel to use the bathroom.

"I need to go too!" she shouted, and took off after him before Mrs. Vanden Boom could reply.

The twins bounded into the building and hid in the business center on the ground floor. With a pencil poised in her hand, Kensy only had to wait a few seconds. This time she scribbled the dots and dashes while Max watched on. When she'd finished, the children looked at each other and then at the page.

In Rome. Following a lead. Will try to see you.
Love, Mum and Dad.

"Max," Kensy gasped, her eyes filling with tears, "they're here."

CHAPTER 18

J⁷⁷∩ FⅬⅬⅣⅬⅉⅭ

Nico Vitale's head was heavy — as if he'd been asleep for days. No matter how hard he willed his eyes to open, it was as though they were disconnected from his brain. He felt as if he was being carried somewhere, cradled like a small child. There was the smell of sweat mixed with cigarettes and cheap cologne. They were going downstairs. The air was colder — much colder than the cloying mustiness of the previous room. He just wanted to go home. Maybe that was where the man was taking him — to his mother and stepfather, to his warm bed and Trisola's delicious meals. How could he have done this to his mamma? She was so busy and he just wanted her to notice him. To love him the way she used to before she met Lorenzo and decided that the whole of Italy needed her more than her own son. He didn't even know if his grandfather would have wanted to see him – that was a fantasy, a distant memory of a man who had once loved him very much.

Nico heard the squeaking of a door.

"You will be safe here until your mother decides to do the right thing and then you will be allowed to go," the man said. "And I promise, if you attempt to escape, it will not end well."

Nico tried to speak, but the words wouldn't come. The last thing he remembered before now was eating soup. It wasn't as good as Trisola's, but it filled his belly and almost straightaway he'd become sleepy. He had no idea how much time had passed, but he recalled the tolling of church bells.

The man lowered Nico onto a bed. This

time the mattress was hard as a rock, but the blankets were warm and he snuggled down. If only he could wake from this nightmare, he would surely find his way back home.

* * *

Max pushed back the covers and tiptoed to the window, which looked out over the Trevi Fountain. Even at half past two in the morning, there were still tourists wandering about taking photographs and tossing coins. He wished that his parents had said more. What was the lead they were following, and what – or who – were they looking for? Knowing they were here in Rome was almost worse than thinking they were thousands of miles away.

In the room directly above him, Kensy was wide-awake too. She'd been going over the message, trying to make sense of it and wondering whether she and Max would get to see their parents. Autumn hadn't asked her anything more about the watch, which she'd found surprising given that she wouldn't have been able to help herself if the shoe was on the other foot. She wondered if Autumn was just being super professional or maybe she was waiting for the right moment. Kensy needed to talk to Max – he'd know what to say. Autumn was so clever – she'd probably worked out that it was Morse code. Kensy wished she didn't have to keep it a secret anymore. It would make life a lot easier.

Kensy peered into the street below. A fancy Italian sports car was parked out in front of the orphanage. She loved Ferraris, while Max preferred Aston Martins. Kensy thought Ferrari engineering was more interesting. While the twins had often joked that one day they'd both drive the cars of their dreams, that never seemed remotely possible until now. She could imagine the Ferrari was the sort of vehicle their Uncle Rupert would be very comfortable in. She couldn't help thinking that he was something of a conundrum – moody one minute then bags of fun the next. Hopefully, she and Max would get to know him a lot better in the coming months and they'd find out who the real Rupert Spencer was.

The door to the orphanage swung open and a woman walked out. She had long dark hair and wore skinny jeans and a tight leather jacket with heels so high Kensy marveled that she could even stand upright in them. Kensy watched as a man in a pinstriped suit got out of the black sports car and embraced her. There was something vaguely familiar about him. He then walked around to the passenger side of the car while the woman hopped into the driver's seat. The engine revved loudly and in a second they were gone.

From the floor below, Max had also seen the car. It was gorgeous. He wondered when he and Kensy would get another opportunity to test their driving skills – with any luck, the car wouldn't try to kill them next time. At least there hadn't been any mishaps during the past few days. But if there was one thing Max had learned since entering the world of Pharos, complacency was a trap he wasn't about to fall into.

CHAPTER 19

7ΠD LU<WEEDΠΛ

"No!" Mr. Reffell held up his shield to defend himself from the hordes of tourists trying to take a photograph with him. "No more pictures, please. We're in a hurry!"

The man extricated an old lady from his waist and wriggled free from another's grasp.

"Do you really think it was a good idea to dress up as a Roman centurion, sir?" Alfie said.

Monty Reffell straightened his helmet and threw his cloak over his shoulder. "Yes, it's a perfectly good idea and you'll thank me once we get to the Colosseum. You'll see. There's method in my madness."

"I thought there was just madness in his madness," Autumn whispered to Kensy, who giggled.

"You should've charged all those people who've been stopping us for photos, sir, you'd have made a fortune," Dante said.

Elliot Frizzle smirked in agreement. Unlike Monty Reffell, whose choice of outfit fell squarely into the category of costume, Elliot looked rather sharp this morning in a raspberry-colored suit paired with navy suede shoes and a matching fedora. He could easily have passed as one of the stylish locals, which Mr. Reffell might have been aiming at but only if it were a thousand years ago.

Monty rolled his eyes and bustled forward, picking up the pace in the hopes that they'd be able to tackle the last half a mile without any further disruptions.

Romilly Vanden Boom had almost choked on her cornflakes when the man arrived at breakfast, though that extra suitcase that clanked and thumped each time it had been moved now made complete sense. She did concede it was a magnificent costume and even better than the one he'd worn while promoting the trip at the school assembly. Lottie Ziegler was very glad he hadn't conned her into dressing up this time too – she didn't mind it at school, but in public was a whole other ball game. You never knew when you might meet someone interesting or madly handsome.

The walk from the hotel to the ancient amphitheater should have taken around half an hour, however, with all the interruptions, it was almost twice as long before they rounded the corner near the magnificent Altare della Patria, which commemorated Victor Emmanuelle, the first unifying leader of Italy. With its bronze horses and winged chariot drivers atop the giant semicircular marble structure, the children couldn't help but gasp.

"That building is seriously stunning," Sachin mumbled, to the nods of his classmates.

"And that one is even *more* amazing!" Yasmina pointed down the road at the Colosseum in the distance.

"Rome is like taking a trip in a time machine." Inez sighed. "It's everything I'd hoped for and so much more."

The smile on Monty Reffell's face couldn't have been any wider as they continued along the road, past the temples and ruins and the incongruous new metro station. Being a lover of history, and knowing that his students had caught the bug too, was incredibly gratifying.

"Why don't they fix more things up?" Lola asked, sweeping her arm in a wide arc. "It's all so old and crumbly. You'd think they'd want it to look nice for the tourists."

Monty blanched. "Lola, these buildings and monuments are constantly under repair."

"Well, they don't do a very good job then," the girl replied.

Misha shook her head vigorously. "No, not a very good job at all," she parroted.

She was so convincing that Kensy almost told her off, which made her stop to wonder whether she should scold Misha in an effort to keep up the whole pretense. It was all a bit confusing. Kensy decided to leave it for another time.

As the group drew closer to the Colosseum, they realized that the crowd was enormous. Against the backdrop of the imposing structure, it had been hard to tell exactly how many people were about. Romilly and Elliot disappeared among the throng to fetch their tickets. Meanwhile, the children arranged themselves in various configurations for pictures in front of the amphitheater with their very own centurion.

"So why *did* you dress up, sir?" Alfie asked.

"See those men there?" Monty pointed at another group of soldiers. "They earn their living by harassing tourists, taking pictures with them and then demanding obscene amounts of money. I heard the going rate is fifty euros. It's highway robbery!"

"Wouldn't they be upset with you encroaching on their turf?" Max asked. He could see four men pointing their way and none of them looked very happy.

"Too bad. I don't mind if they harass everyone else, but I want them to leave us alone and my tactic seems to be working perfectly well." Monty nodded, feeling pretty pleased with himself.

Except that it wasn't working well at all. The four men had now become eight and they were clearly about to make themselves known.

Carlos pointed over Mr. Reffell's shoulder. "Sir."

"What's the matter, Rodriguez?" The man turned and, before he could say another word, one of the burly gladiators jabbed a stubby finger in the center of his chest.

"*Cosa fai?*" the man spat.

Monty gulped. "Dressing up for the children," he replied. "It's not against the law."

"That is *our* domain," another man shouted, waving his fist in the air.

"Well, I don't see I'm doing any harm," Monty said, right before the burliest member of the group grabbed him by the throat. Monty began to make choking noises, ostensibly in the hope that his attacker would release him.

He wasn't supposed to retaliate in front of the children, but if the fellow didn't desist soon, he would be left with little choice – and there was a part of him that was itching to have a go. "Please," he coughed. "That is very unpleasant."

Kensy marched forward and stamped heavily on the perpetrator's sandaled foot. "Let Mr. Reffell go!" she demanded.

The man yelped in pain and released his grip, then began jumping around, clutching his injured toe. The rest of the children were stunned but mostly impressed.

Monty Reffell drew his plastic sword. "I challenge you to a duel!" he cried, and was met with laughter. "I don't see what's so funny. I am an excellent swordsman."

"*Stupido*," the shortest of the group said, chuckling.

"I am not *stupido*, I can guarantee you that," Mr. Reffell said, drawing himself up to full height.

Max spotted a policeman and nudged Autumn. "I think perhaps we need to defuse this, don't you?"

Autumn nodded. "Good thinking."

They took off across the piazza.

"*Mi scusi!*" Max called to the uniformed man. Then, with a fair amount of arm waving and grammatically incorrect Italian, he managed to tell the officer exactly what was going on – except that he might have left out the bit about his teacher dressing up as a centurion to try to outsmart the actors. "Those men over there are demanding a fortune for a photograph and we're just innocent children," Max blurted.

The policeman was off after them like a shot. Although the centurions weren't doing anything illegal, as they were registered street performers, the constabulary were stationed around the building to protect tourists from being ripped off and it sounded as if the children were being held for ransom.

"*Allontanatevi dai bambini!* Get away from the children!" the policeman shouted, sending the centurions scattering.

Mr. Reffell rubbed his neck, wishing that just once he might be able to put all those years of martial arts training to good use.

Unfortunately, it was against company policy unless absolutely necessary. A good old sword fight would have sufficed. He then spent several minutes trying to explain to the officer that he was with the children. Even then, it didn't stop the policeman from issuing him an on-the-spot penalty for not having a permit to dress as an ancient figure in a public place.

Luckily, Mrs. Vanden Boom and Mr. Frizzle appeared with the tickets and their guide, a middle-aged woman with a pixie cut and a powerful voice. As the children followed their teachers through the entrance, Kensy looked up and gasped.

"Max!" she shouted, charging toward her brother. She knocked him sideways to the ground as a stone the size of a car battery shattered onto the ground, sending the tourists scrambling. Carlos and Autumn ran to Max's aid as the rest of the group disappeared inside the Flavian amphitheater. Kensy stood up and dusted herself off.

"Are you two okay?" Autumn gasped.

Max's heart was pounding, but he wasn't

hurt. The stone had hit the ground exactly where he'd been standing moments before.

Kensy stared up at the building. For a second she thought she'd seen a face in one of the openings, but then it was gone.

Carlos offered Max his arm.

Inside the Colosseum, Lottie Ziegler had done a quick head count and realized there were four students missing. She hurried back to the entrance and was surprised to see Carlos helping Max to his feet and rubble on the ground around him.

"What happened?" she asked urgently, looking left and right.

Max stood up and scratched his head.

Kensy had no idea why she'd looked up when she did. Luck maybe? A mere coincidence? Perhaps she'd heard something and didn't realize it. She hated to think about what shape her brother would be in if she hadn't seen that stone. Kensy licked her lips and swallowed hard. "I think someone just tried to kill Max."

CHAPTER 20

ᒧᑌᑎ᠊ᒧᑌ

"*That* was amazing," Dante said.

"Terrifying, did you say?" Autumn shook her head. Kensy could only agree with her friend.

"You weren't really bothered by what Madiana told us, were you?" The boy frowned. He'd never known Autumn to be squeamish. Dante had enjoyed everything about the tour and particularly that their guide hadn't held back on the gruesome stories. She'd told them all about the lions tearing men from limb to limb, gladiators impaled on the horns of marauding rhinoceroses and sacrifices of young women to appease the gods.

"No, not that," Autumn said. "The fact that someone tried to kill Max."

Kensy had barely listened to a word while they were inside. She was too busy trying to remember what the person had looked like and searching for their face among the tourists. Really, though, she had no idea – it had all happened so fast.

Mrs. Vanden Boom and Miss Ziegler had both done their best to convince the children that it was just an accident, but Kensy was having none of it – not after what had happened in London. Why did someone want to harm them? Did it have something to do with their grandmother or their parents?

"I am sure that it was merely a freak accident," Mr. Reffell said to Kensy and Autumn, as they made their way to lunch. "Construction commenced on the Colosseum in 72 AD – it's even older than me, if you can believe it – and the metal struts used to hold it together were removed centuries ago as was most of the marble, which was pillaged to help construct St. Peter's Basilica over at the Vatican. I'm afraid there have been quite a few near misses over the years, and wasn't Max fortunate that Kensy spotted the falling stone and pushed him out of the way?"

Max could only agree with that. He really didn't want to believe that it was anything other than bad luck – or good luck, as it turned out.

"Anyway, I don't know about the rest of you, but I'm starving," the teacher said. He hoped their afternoon at the Roman Forum would be less eventful, having also lost Misha and Lola inside for almost half an hour.

Thankfully, Romilly had located the pair playing with a litter of kittens in a cordoned-off area that was under repair. Lola had thrown a hissy fit when the teacher requested she remove one of the creatures from her pocket. Their tour guide, Madiana, said there were over one hundred and twenty thousand feral felines living in the city's monuments, and more than three hundred of them were inside the Colosseum itself. That didn't appease Lola, who couldn't imagine anyone would miss one little puss.

As the group crossed the road toward their lunch venue, Kensy was distracted from her thoughts by a display of daily newspapers outside a small kiosk. She nudged Autumn and pointed. "Look."

Yasmina and Inez were walking with the girls and saw it too. The front pages of all the papers carried the same picture of a man and woman standing on either side of a young boy whose face was angled toward his mother and partly obscured. One headline read "Nico is Home." Another screamed "Runaway Returns."

Yasmina smiled. "What a relief for his poor parents."

"Absolutely," Kensy agreed.

"Well, that's one less thing for the woman to be worried about," Romilly commented. "She's got enough on her plate, what with the grain shortage."

"Is it really that bad?" Autumn asked.

"Apparently so," the woman replied. She had taken it upon herself to do some research last night. "From what I understand, Vittoria Vitale passed a law last year prohibiting the importation of grain in order to protect the Italian farmers. It was wildly unpopular with their international trading partners, but the locals were ecstatic. Unfortunately, since then there has been a slew of disasters with wheat crops failing all over the country. Odd occurrences, such as unseasonal fires and beetle infestations, have resulted in a severe grain shortage, which is pushing up the prices."

"Why can't they reverse the law and buy their wheat from overseas again?" Inez asked. It seemed the most obvious thing to do, but then world affairs weren't her strong suit.

Romilly looked at the girl. "Italian politics is far more complicated than that, I'm afraid. I'm sure the woman rues the day she made the decision, but, in order to rescind, she needs a seventy-five percent majority of her fellow parliamentarians and that's highly unlikely given that the very idea of protectionism has been something many politicians have been arguing in favor of for years."

"Politics is such a dreary business," Kensy said. "I'd hate to be in charge of a country — that's way too much responsibility." As the words came out of her mouth, her mind turned to Cordelia and what a huge job her grandmother had. If you were a politician, you could get voted out of office or retire. Once you were part of Pharos, you were in it for life — unless there were extenuating circumstances. Even then, Kensy and Max had ended up back in the business their parents had tried to leave behind.

The group reached the restaurant and were quickly seated at a sunny table beneath a trellis with a naked grapevine. The maître d' had been expecting them. Lottie Ziegler studied the menu and blinked twice when she registered the prices.

"All right, kids, order up," Monty instructed cheerfully. "Pizza, pasta, whatever you like — this place is one of the best." He beckoned a waiter over to their table. "I'll have a margherita pizza, please, and a side of cannelloni. Oh, and where are the bread baskets for the table?" the man asked. "These children might devour the tablecloths if you don't bring something soon."

"*Sì, signore*," the man said, and scurried away.

"Are you sure about that, Monty?" Elliot Frizzle called from the other end of the table.

"Yes, of course," the man said with a nod. "The children have to eat."

"But are you certain you want them to order for themselves?" Mr. Frizzle asked.

"They're not babies," Monty replied. "They can decide what they want. I'd rather that than having a whole lot of whining if they don't like my choices."

Lottie and Romilly looked at each other, having both realized why Elliot was asking.

"It's on his head," Romilly whispered to her colleague.

Lottie grinned. "Or his credit card."

And while, as Monty had forecast, lunch was absolutely delicious, the man almost had a stroke when he saw the bill.

* * *

"Please, sir, can we catch a bus back to the hotel?" Alfie begged. "I'm exhausted." Everyone else was feeling the same way after three hours of traipsing through the ruins of the Roman Forum.

"No, we can't afford it and if I can keep walking with this," Mr. Reffell said, pulling down the top of his left sock to reveal a blister the size of Spain on his heel, "then you can manage it too."

Alfie made a face. "Geez, that's gross, sir."

There was a murmur of agreement from the rest of the children.

"Not as gross as wearing socks with sandals," Harper whispered to Yasmina.

Monty ignored the girl. It might not have been traditional according to his centurion outfit, but he simply couldn't abide cold feet and it was bad enough having his knees exposed.

Kensy was walking with Max, lagging a little behind everyone else. They had barely had a second together since receiving the message from their parents last night, never mind this morning's incident. While they loved being

215

with their friends and the trip was fantastic so far, they were craving some time alone. Up ahead of them, Misha and Lola were still carrying on about the cats and Lola was clearly holding a grudge against Mrs. Vanden Boom for making her leave the kitten behind.

"Are you okay?" Kensy asked her brother.

Max nodded. "I'm fine, and you should stop jumping to conclusions. Like Reff said, it was an accident."

Kensy shrugged. "Well, if you want to think that, I can't stop you."

"I need to," Max said, glancing across at his sister.

"Okay – I'll stop going on about it. But we have to stick together," Kensy said, her voice foundering for a second. "I couldn't deal with anything happening to you too."

Max wrapped an arm around her shoulders and gave her a squeeze.

"You don't have to strangle me," she said, pushing him away. He grinned in return and a moment later she leaned her head against his. "I do love you, Max, even if you are a pain sometimes," she whispered, before running off to join Autumn and the others. Max chased after her, catching up with Carlos.

The streets alternated between narrow cobbled roads and broad piazzas. The children approached Quirinal Palace, which Mr. Reffell explained was the residence of the Italian president, who was both statesman and figure-head, elected by the people and in charge of making sure that the government did the right thing. The prime minister, on the other hand, was the leader of the parliament.

As they neared the building, three black cars with dark tinted windows whizzed past at speed – a Range Rover in front, followed by a huge Mercedes Benz, then another Range Rover at the rear. A wide set of gates opened and the vehicles zoomed through into a central courtyard inside the palace. The children heard shouts and angry voices as they neared the opening.

Although Mr. Reffell continued on his way, several of the group stopped to have a look. Max and Carlos peered inside and were spotted by a lump of a fellow who raised his head ever so slightly. Carlos gave a wave just as the man pulled back his jacket to reveal a shoulder holster. The grin on his face settled into a sneer and the boys hurried away.

"Did you see that?" Carlos whispered. "Glock, nine millimeter."

Max, who had been studying firearms in some detail lately, thought it was too. "Probably one of the president's bodyguards."

"He's mean looking; I wouldn't want to cross him," Carlos said as the shouting intensified.

Further back along the line, Lola was still banging on about the cat. Misha turned her head but didn't flinch when she realized who was doing most of the yelling. Although she'd never met the man in person, she'd spent a lot of time studying his photographs. A short fellow with a paunch and a pronounced Roman nose, his hair had receded completely from the top of his head and sat like a half-eaten donut at the back and sides. He was gesticulating wildly at a young fellow who had his head down, muttering a stream of apologies.

"What are you gawking at?" Lola said. She

turned and glanced into the courtyard just as the man stormed out of view.

"Italians are so passionate, aren't they?" Misha said, trying to divert the girl's attention. "Always yelling and talking with their hands." She gave what was meant to be a funny demonstration, but Lola didn't laugh. Instead the girl looked quite put off.

"What's wrong with that?" Lola snapped, her eyes narrowing. Two deep frown lines appeared at the top of her nose.

Misha gulped. "Nothing."

Lola stared at Misha, then flicked her hair over her shoulder and launched into another tirade about the cat.

Misha wondered if Lola had seen the man. If she had, she certainly wasn't saying so. Misha needed to get a message to Dame Spencer and fast. Sergio Leonardi's appearance at Quirinal Palace had changed the game completely. But with the active Pharos agents already engaged in a top secret mission on the other side of the world, perhaps this time the responsibility was about to fall elsewhere.

CHAPTER 21

⁊⅃⌐⌐⌐ ⣷⣿ ⣷⣿⌐⣷⣿⌐⣷⣿

"Can I use your room for a minute?" Misha whispered to Autumn and Kensy.

The two girls looked at her curiously. They hadn't so much as stepped through the hotel doors when Lola bounded away upstairs, eager to get changed out of her uniform. Mrs. Vanden Boom had told the children they could spend the rest of the day in casual clothes, so Lola had important decisions to make – being stylish in Rome wasn't an option, it was mandatory. Misha had begged off for a moment, telling the girl she was feeling a bit unwell and wanted to see if Mrs. Vanden Boom had some laxatives. She knew Lola wouldn't want to be part of *that* conversation.

"Of course," Autumn said. "Is there anything we can help with?"

"I just need to check in. I saw something earlier and I think it might be important," Misha said.

"Won't Lola be wondering where you are?" Kensy asked.

"She'll be ages getting changed and this should only take a few minutes." Misha smiled tightly. Ever since she'd seen Sergio, her mind had been going a million miles a minute.

Kensy handed over her key. "Here, take this. Good luck."

Kensy and Autumn exchanged quizzical looks, but they weren't about to ask Misha what she'd seen. Her mission with Lola was highly classified and, until they needed to know, it was really none of their business.

"Mrs. Vanden Boom said there were some snacks upstairs," Kensy said. Lunch seemed a long time ago and dinner wasn't until six.

The girls headed upstairs to the restaurant, where there were platters of fruit and some biscotti. Kensy made two cups of tea and the pair sat in the window, watching the crowds in the piazza below. The fountain was every bit as popular as it was yesterday.

"Do you think Mr. Frizzle would be willing to take us for a walk somewhere?" Kensy said. She hated the idea of being cooped up inside until dinner.

The room was filling fast with hungry children, chattering about the day. Max walked up behind his sister. He and Carlos had already ditched their uniforms, and Autumn was secretly admiring Max's navy sweater. The color really brought out the blue of his eyes.

"Frizzle wants to look at some art gallery around the corner, if you're keen to get out," Max said. "But he's leaving in ten minutes, so you'd better hurry up."

"Seriously, can you two read each other's minds?" Autumn said with a grin, and downed the last dregs of her tea.

"Meet you at the front door," Kensy said to the boys as she and Autumn dashed away to get changed.

* * *

"Now, I know you're all very reliable and, with Max's memory for maps, you're welcome to take a spin around the block for half an hour so long as you stay together," Elliot Frizzle said to the children. They were standing outside the entrance to the gallery, which was located around the corner from the hotel. He had been dying to pop by ever since he'd noticed a stunning print of a lion in the window yesterday. If it wasn't too expensive, he had exactly the right spot for it in his apartment.

"Thanks, Mr. Frizzle," Max said, glancing at his watch. "We'll meet you back here in thirty minutes."

Elliot rubbed his hands together gleefully. He'd just glimpsed a bronze relief of Caesar that would look divine on the side table in his entrance hall.

"Have fun, sir," Carlos said.

"Oh, I will – don't you worry about that, young man." He smiled broadly then dipped his hat and pushed open the shop door, tripping a tinkly bell that alerted the owner to his arrival.

The children set off along the street, with Autumn pointing out the amazing array of door knockers that ranged from intertwined vipers to lion's heads and goddesses.

"They're a bit boring, though," Carlos said, "unless you use them." He ran to the nearest door and gave the knocker a loud pounding. The noise made the rest of them jump.

Max grimaced. "Really?"

Carlos began to run. "Come on," he called over his shoulder.

The other three raced after the lad just as the door opened and a man with a moustache poked his head out into the street, looking perplexed. They turned the corner, puffing.

"You shouldn't have done that," Autumn chided over the sound of Kensy's giggles.

"It was only for a laugh," Carlos said. "Seriously, Autumn, sometimes I think you're a card-carrying member of the fun police."

The girl eyeballed the lad. "It's not *that* funny. Besides, the man might have been in the middle of something important."

"Whatever," Carlos said, waving a hand in the air.

"Where are we?" Kensy took in their surroundings. The trouble was that lots of the streets and alleys looked the same.

"The other side of the orphanage," Max said.

Up ahead, a door opened and a man dressed in a dark waistcoat, gray shirt and black pants walked outside. He pulled a cigarette from his pocket and lit it, kicking at the cobbles while he blew smoke rings into the air. He sat down on the top step, oblivious to their presence.

"We should go," Max said.

Just as they were about to turn back, three boys and two girls ran around the corner. Kensy realized she'd seen the tallest of the lads yesterday. He was the kid she'd thought had stolen the man's wallet near the Spanish Steps. Except that he hadn't – or maybe he had. She was still confused about what had actually happened. There was something else about him too, but she couldn't put her finger on it.

The man stood up and walked back inside the building. He reappeared with a wicker laundry basket and dumped it on the ground. *"Cosa avete portato?"* he said, taking a drag of his cigarette and glaring at the children.

"What did he say?" Autumn whispered to Kensy. Instinctively, the four of them had stepped behind a car.

"What did you bring?" Kensy replied, her eyes widening as it soon became clear. The five children emptied their pockets and backpacks, a veritable avalanche of wallets and purses, phones, cameras and money raining into the basket.

"I feel like we've stumbled into the pages of a Charles Dickens novel," Max whispered as he peered out from behind the hatchback that was shielding them from view.

The man threw his cigarette onto the ground and stubbed it out, then picked up the basket. *"Ottimo lavoro."* He grinned, revealing a glinting gold tooth. "There will be thousands out there tonight for the marches. Go, go!"

The five children turned and ran away, back down the lane. Who knew where they would find their next victims and how many there had already been that day.

"Come on," Kensy said. "We've got to tell the police."

Just as they were about to leave, the man with the basket spotted them. "Hey!" he called out. "What are you looking at?"

He took a step inside the door, then barked something unintelligible in Italian. But his meaning soon became clear as three younger men stormed out into the street.

"Get them!" the older fellow shouted.

Max grabbed his sister's hand and the four of them took off. But the men were fast and hot on their heels.

"This way!" Max yelled, leading them around the corner and into a narrow lane, where cars were whizzing through. The boy was trying to remember the layout of the area from the map he'd studied. He was frantically thinking about how they could double back to the hotel.

Carlos followed Max across the road, right in front of a speeding car. It screeched to a halt, gently coming to rest against the boy's leg. Carlos grabbed Autumn's hand and the pair leapt over the hood as the driver beeped his horn and shook his fist. The three thugs were still coming at them. One of them ran straight into the car door. He bounced off, grabbing the side mirror, which came away in his hand.

Max felt as if his chest was about to explode. "Up here!" he yelled. "Hurry!"

The children reached the end of the road and were suddenly caught in a wave of people chanting and waving placards. It seemed that last night's protesters had swollen tenfold, and the angry men and women had taken over the streets. Max wound his way through the crowd, clutching his sister's hand, but as hard as they tried to stick together, they were soon separated. Max's voice was drowned out by the shouting and he had no idea where Kensy had disappeared to. Among the sea of faces, he spotted Autumn being jostled behind him, but there was no sign of Carlos. He could only hope that Kensy was forging on. Max was heading toward Autumn when he stopped dead and swallowed air.

"Dad!" the boy screamed. He dodged the oncoming throng, his shouts rising higher and higher. For a second, he forgot all about the men pursuing them. Max's cries caught in his throat as he lost sight of his father. "Dad, where are you?" he screamed again, turning circles among the mass, hot tears pricking at his eyes.

A pair of thick arms reached out and grabbed him. Instinctively, Max kicked backward, connecting with the fellow's shin hard enough that he released his grip. Max dove under a nearby pair of legs like a rugby player, then scrambled to his feet and ran as fast as he could. He almost crashed into Autumn, who grabbed his hand and wrenched him sideways. They held on tight and dashed in and out of the demonstrators until they reached a building on the edge of the road, where they pressed themselves into the doorway and out of sight. It was only then that Max let go. He wiped his face with the backs of his hands.

"Are you okay?" she asked.

Max closed his eyes and nodded.

"There's Kensy!" Autumn waved her arms and screamed as loudly as she could, but the girl was running ahead and didn't hear her.

Fortunately, Carlos had located Max and Autumn. He reached them, puffing and panting. "I think we lost them," he called over the chanting, which had now combined with whistles and drums. There were fiery torches too.

Autumn shook her head and pointed. "No, there they are – right behind Kensy."

The boys looked at each other. They had to cause a distraction so Kensy would get away, but how they were going to make themselves heard over this din was anyone's guess. Then Max remembered something. "My watch has a loudspeaker on it – Mrs. Vanden Boom showed me the other day."

"Well, hurry up and use it!" Carlos urged.

Max fiddled with the contraption. There was a screech of feedback then the boy's voice boomed, "Pickpockets! *Borseggiatori!*" The crowd was briefly silenced. Carlos had climbed up a drainpipe and was pointing at the men who were dodging their way through the melee.

Kensy looked around and spotted Carlos with her brother and Autumn. She ran toward them. Almost immediately, the mob began to jostle the fellows while some of the protestors made a grab for them. The ruckus impeded their progress just long enough for the children to make their escape.

Max pointed to a small alley. "This way!"

"It better not be a dead end," Kensy panted. She turned to look back and saw that the thugs had also emerged from the crowd and were after them again.

The children fled down the alley.

"The hotel's on the other side of that building," Max said.

"There's a gate!" Kensy yelled.

Autumn grabbed the metal posts and rattled them fiercely. "It's locked!"

Kensy foraged around in her messy hair, pulling out her hair clip along with several long blonde strands. She fumbled, trying to get the device into the ancient padlock.

"Hurry, they're coming!" Autumn urged.

Finally, the mechanism gave way and the gate swung open. The children rushed through.

"Close it!" Max shouted.

One of the men reached the gate and was pushing hard, but the kids threw their weight against the metal so that Kensy could snap the lock shut. The other two men arrived just as she did, and it was clear from their size that the children would have stood no chance against the three of them.

Max stared into one of the men's ink-colored eyes. His chin was covered in stubble and there was a deep scar across his left cheek. He had a small tattoo on his wrist – Max thought it said "hero." That was a joke. There was certainly nothing heroic about this guy.

"*Sei morto*," the man called after the children as they fled down a steep set of stairs and into the cellar below.

CHAPTER 22

ᒪᗝᒐᐱ ᐱᒐᒍᒷᔈᗝᗝ

"So where are we?" Carlos asked, his question bouncing around the walls of the dark space. It seemed they had entered a musty basement.

"Shh!" Autumn pressed her finger to her lips.

Max fiddled with his watch until a glow illuminated the room. Judging by the domed ceiling, crucifixes and statues of Jesus and the Madonna, they had to be in the church near the Trevi Fountain.

"Do you think Sister Maria Regina knows the children in her orphanage are a gang of thieves?" Kensy said.

Autumn frowned. "You'd hope not. Maybe those men make the children do it and she has no idea."

"We need to tell the police as soon as we get out of here," Max said. "And we'd better get a move on or Frizzle will never let us go anywhere alone again."

The children began hunting around for a way out. Toward the end of the room was a narrow staircase that spiraled upward.

"What if they're waiting for us outside?" Carlos said.

"Well," Max reasoned, "if I've got the right church, and I'm pretty sure I do, it's just across the piazza from the hotel and there'll still be hundreds of people around. We should be able to make it."

The children ascended the stairs into a small room. Max peered out through the red velvet fabric that formed a vestibule hiding the access point. They were standing at the side of a magnificent altar. Overhead were stunning frescos and ornate plasterwork, and a vast array of gleaming brass crosses on the walls.

"Is anyone out there?" Kensy mouthed to her brother.

"A nun," he whispered.

"Let me see." Kensy pulled back the curtain and saw the woman. She was walking down the aisle on the far side and turned to genuflect before hurrying away via the front doors.

"That was Sister Maria Regina," Kensy said. "I'd recognize that nose anywhere. Come on, she's gone."

Just as the children were about to step out of their hiding spot, they heard the sound of heels clacking on the marble floor.

Carlos groaned. "We're never going to get out of here."

A woman, dressed from head to toe in black with a veil covering her face, entered one of the middle pews. She knelt down and bowed her head.

"What should we do?" Kensy hissed.

Max pointed to the passageways on either side of the pews. If they were quiet, and the woman kept praying, they should be able to make it past without her noticing. They were about to make a dash for it when the woman began to weep.

"Dear Father in Heaven," she wailed, "please bring my son back to me. He is a good boy."

A priest appeared from nowhere, his footsteps soundless, but the woman was immediately aware of his presence and raised her head. She crossed herself and stood up to greet him, wiping the tears from beneath her veil with a small handkerchief.

"*Primo Ministro*," he said, taking her hands in his, "you are giving thanks for the return of Nico."

The woman nodded her head fiercely. "The Lord is good."

Autumn nudged Kensy, and Max did the same to Carlos.

"She's the prime minister," Max whispered. "She was just praying for the return of her son, but the newspapers say he's home. What's that all about?"

Autumn frowned. "Maybe he's home in body but not in spirit? He could be difficult – after all, he did run away in the first place."

The children willed the pair to wrap things up and leave. They had about two minutes to meet Mr. Frizzle at the gallery or they'd be in big trouble.

"Let me walk with you," the priest offered.

Prime Minister Vitale raised a finger in the air. "One more minute, please. I would like to speak with our heavenly Father."

"Of course, *signora*. I will leave you in private and meet you at the rear entrance, where I presume your car is waiting." The priest disappeared into one of the wings.

The children watched as the woman pulled a folded piece of paper from her handbag. She walked to the side of the church and stood by a marble urn. They were surprised to see her lift the lid and drop the page inside. She knelt and genuflected toward the altar, then hurried away in the same direction the priest had gone. Only when the children heard a door creaking did they flee from their hiding place.

Carlos was just about to take a peek outside

when he realized that Kensy wasn't with them. He was shocked to see her standing next to the urn, its lid off and her hand inside.

"What are you doing?" Max hissed.

"Taking a picture. It might be important," she said, unfolding the piece of paper and laying it on the floor. She used her watch to snap a close-up photograph. By the time Autumn had reached her, she'd already finished and was about to drop the paper back into the urn.

"What was it?" the girl asked.

"No time now," Kensy said as she heard whistling. Someone was coming.

Carlos opened the door. The crowd near the fountain was even bigger than before and there was no sign of the three thugs. Still, they would have to make a dash for the gallery around the corner and hope that Mr. Frizzle hadn't left yet. "Follow me," the boy said, and the four of them bolted down the front steps and into the crowd.

The priest looked up as he heard the door close. He was sure he had locked it earlier — it would not do well for the prime minister to be mingling with the general public at the moment. They were already baying for her blood and the lines at the soup kitchen were getting longer each day. There was talk in the newspapers of flour rationing. The biggest pasta supplier in the country, Penina, which was owned by the government, had raised its prices three times in the past month. Italy was headed for disaster if the crisis wasn't averted soon.

The children ran around the corner, past the hotel entrance and pulled up outside the gallery. Carlos pressed his face against the window, but the store was empty.

"He's gone," the boy said. "And we're dead."

Autumn had a look too. She thought she saw some movement at the rear of the shops and broke into a grin at the sight of Mr. Frizzle and the sales assistant emerging from a back room. "He's still inside."

Elliot Frizzle heard the clock on the wall chiming the quarter hour and realized that he'd taken far longer than he'd anticipated. The children had probably returned to the hotel by now, but as he glanced toward the street, there they were — as reliable as ever.

He rushed to the door. "Sorry, kids, this place is a treasure trove – it goes on for miles! I've just been arranging to have some things sent home to London, but would you mind helping me carry a few things I can pack in my suitcase?" The man grimaced. His credit card had taken a beating and then some.

"Of course, sir," the group echoed.

"I hope you haven't been too bored. I know I told you to stay close and you're probably sick to death of watching the tourists," the man said as the children followed him around to the hotel. They were carrying an assortment of antiquities, including a Roman soldier's helmet, an ancient pot and a Venetian glass vase.

"No, it's been really . . . interesting," Max said.

"So much excitement you couldn't imagine it, sir," Carlos added.

Kensy and Autumn nodded.

Elliot Frizzle paused to look at the children. "Oh, thank you for making me feel better. I shouldn't have left you so long." He hoped they were telling the truth. He'd take them out for a ramble after dinner and this time they'd go somewhere interesting.

CHAPTER 23

LWJOJ ΛDEEJ7DE

The children helped carry Mr. Frizzle's haul up to his room on the second floor before he suggested they'd best go and get ready for dinner – it was already twenty to six. But the kids had other ideas. They were dying to see the photo Kensy had taken, and it also occurred to Autumn that they hadn't yet told the police about the pickpockets either.

"See you soon, sir." Carlos gave a wave and the four of them flew upstairs to Kensy and Autumn's room. They would most likely be left alone up there, although the hotel did seem unusually quiet. Perhaps the rest of the teachers had taken their groups out too – either that or they were all having a siesta.

Once they were safely inside, Kensy pulled out her watch and projected the note onto the wall above their beds. Max quickly copied it down on a piece of paper. At first glance, it looked like gobbledygook, but Max soon realized it was a code. Except this time it wasn't as simple as the Caesar cipher.

"I'll work on it until we have to go to dinner," Max said.

"I'll help, if you like," Autumn offered. She and Max had both tied for first place in their code-breaking class during training last week.

"That would be great, thanks," Max said. "I've never seen anything quite like it before and you're brilliant, so, between the two of us, I'm sure we'll crack it."

Autumn could feel the blush rising to her cheeks. "We can only try."

Kensy was jiggling from one foot to the other. Her brain was in overdrive, thinking about what the prime minister had said in her prayers. "Do you think Nico could have been kidnapped?"

"Anything's possible," Carlos replied. "I mean, he is the son of one of the most important people in the country."

There was something scratching away at the back of Kensy's mind, but whatever it was refused to focus. "Maybe there's a clue in that note." She looked at Max and Autumn, who were already hard at work. "Can you hurry up and solve it?"

"We're doing our best," Max grouched. "Perhaps you could find something useful to do and stop distracting us."

Kensy tapped her foot. "What if Carlos and I report the pickpockets to the police?"

Carlos nodded. "Yeah, let's do that."

Autumn looked up. "Yes, we have to tell the authorities – it's horrible to think about all those people who've lost their belongings. Hopefully, the police can raid the building and return everything to their owners."

"I'm not sure it's a good idea," Max said. "If Frizzle knows you've gone outside without him, he'll be furious and we just managed to avoid getting into trouble with him before — more by good luck than good planning."

Kensy ran to the window and peered into the piazza. She could see three uniformed officers right below them. "Then I'll call to them from the doorway."

"If you think that will work," Max said, returning to the code. "Go for it."

Kensy and Carlos flew down the stairs. Wherever the others had been before, they were back now, as the floors were squeaking, doors were banging and they could hear voices. As they reached the entrance foyer, Mrs. Vanden Boom walked inside with Misha, Lola, Graham and Alfie traipsing after her.

"And where are you two going?" she said sternly, glancing at her watch. "It's almost dinnertime."

"I dropped my itinerary outside," Kensy said. "I saw it from the window, and Carlos is coming with me — it will only take a second."

The woman nodded. "Straight out and back again. If you can't find it, I think I've got a spare."

Misha looked at the pair. There was something in her eyes. Kensy would talk to her later in private – if she could get rid of Lola for longer than ten seconds.

Kensy and Carlos spotted a policeman at the rear of the crowd and raced toward him. In her best Italian, Kensy explained exactly what they had seen in the lane behind the orphanage. The man smiled and told her that she must have been imagining things. Sister Maria Regina's orphans were good children and they were so well cared for that they would never resort to that type of behavior.

Kensy tried again and told him about the three thugs that had chased her and her friends, but the man shook his head.

"Come on, Kensy, it's obvious he doesn't believe you," Carlos said, guiding her by the arm. He glanced at the other side of the fountain and froze.

Kensy pulled away. "Maybe I'm not explaining things properly."

"We have to go," Carlos insisted. "It's dinnertime and someone is watching us."

Kensy's eyes skimmed the crowd of tourists.

"Just turn around and we'll head back inside," he continued. "We can't stay out here. It's too dangerous."

Kensy grudgingly thanked the policeman and walked with Carlos to the hotel door, her heart pounding. She wondered if they should have gone somewhere else because now the brute knew where they were staying.

The pair charged up to the top floor, where Max and Autumn had scattered sheets of paper all over the bed in an effort to decipher the code. Kensy and Carlos ran to the window and looked down into the piazza, but what they saw was even more disturbing than the sneer on that horrible man's face. The young policeman Kensy had been speaking to and the thug were standing together, laughing.

Kensy turned to Carlos. "I hope we're not the joke," she said.

Carlos bit his lip. "I have a bad feeling that we are."

CHAPTER 24

LKJL>∧Jᒣ<

Vittoria Vitale picked at the skin around her perfectly manicured fingernails. She paced up and down the dining room, although food was the furthest thing from her mind. Not only was she in danger of losing Nico forever, her reputation – already in tatters because of the wheat shortage – would be unsalvageable if she gave in to the kidnappers' demands.

"Have you made a decision?" Lorenzo asked as he entered the room.

Vittoria shook her head but did not turn around. "What if they don't even have him?

I have asked for proof of life and then I will decide."

"What is their deadline?" Lorenzo asked.

"Two days," she whispered. "If I tell a soul, they have said Nico will come back to us in tiny pieces."

Lorenzo placed a hand on his wife's shoulder. She spun around and buried her face into his broad chest. "We will get through this, *mia cara*," he said, holding her tightly. "There is no other choice."

Lorenzo Rinaldi closed his eyes. A parcel had arrived for Vittoria that morning, which he had intercepted at the door. He had opened it, not wanting to put her through any more distress. It was a lock of dark curly hair. But what they said they would send next didn't bear thinking about.

* * *

A sliver of light shone through a crack in the ceiling as Nico lay in his bed, watching the dust dance in the air, the particles floating like aimless ballerinas. He could occasionally hear car horns and people shouting. Perhaps they had not taken him from the city. He pushed back the covers and dropped his feet to the floor, willing his jellylike legs to carry him to the door. Nico gripped the handle, but it didn't budge.

"Is anyone there?" he called feebly. His throat was dry, his voice almost nonexistent. "Hello!" he tried again, banging on the door.

"Pipe down!" a man growled from the other side. "Do you want to wake up the whole neighborhood?"

"I'm hungry," Nico said. "And thirsty."

"And ridiculous. There is food and drink inside already. Can you not see it?"

Nico cast his eyes around the room and realized there was a small cupboard on the wall beside the door. He opened it and found a glass of milk and a plate of pasta under a plastic dome. It was still warm. He took them both and sat down on the edge of the bed, practically inhaling the meal.

"*Grazie*," he said, and returned the plate and glass to the little box then closed the door.

There were footsteps outside and the sound of muffled voices. He tiptoed back to the food hatch and opened the door, hoping to hear more despite the cover on the other side being closed.

"She wants proof of life," a woman said. "She will not sign off on the deal until she knows he is alive."

"A photograph?"

"Not just a photograph. There needs to be something in real time in the frame. Television news – it must be current," the woman said.

"Do you want me to take him upstairs?" the man asked.

"Of course not, you nincompoop! He will try to escape. You need to bring a television down here."

Nico's heart sank. For a moment there he thought he had his chance.

"When?" the man said.

"As soon as possible, if she ever wants to see the boy again."

Nico's stomach twisted. He had to find a way out of here and fast.

CHAPTER 25

LOJL>OJ

Autumn yawned and rubbed her tired eyes. She'd finally given up and gone to sleep just after two, but the sound of machinery outside the window had woken her before dawn.

Kensy rolled over in her bed and snuggled down under the covers, trying to block out the noise. "What is that?" she mumbled. She'd been dreaming of her parents and wanted desperately to fall back to sleep.

Autumn hopped out of bed and walked to the window. In the predawn light, she could see three men in chest waders — the sort fishermen wore – standing in the fountain. Two were pushing brooms through the water while the other was holding the end of something that resembled a giant vacuum cleaner. "They're clearing the coins," she said. "Mr. Reffell mentioned they do it three times a week and the money goes to the church to look after homeless people."

Kensy pulled the duvet higher. "Seriously, that machine sounds like a tree mulcher. I'm *so* tired."

After dinner, the children had convinced Mr. Frizzle to have an early night. The man hadn't minded at all, given they had to be up at the crack of dawn to take the train to Pompeii for the day. The four children had returned to Kensy and Autumn's room and spent until lights-out working on the code together without success. Autumn and Kensy had continued their efforts after the boys had left, but many hours later the girls were still nowhere close to solving it.

Autumn was just about to go back to bed when she suddenly noticed something. She squinted to make sure. "Kensy, come here. You need to see this."

The girl's feet hit the floor with a thud. Her mind was still roiling after everything that had happened yesterday. Kensy pushed her hair out of her eyes and walked to the window. The piazza was almost empty save for the men in the pond and a fellow who was pushing up the shutters on a coffee shop.

"Do those guys look familiar to you?" Autumn asked.

Kensy gasped. "They're the thugs who were chasing us. From the orphanage."

Autumn nodded. "That's what I thought."

There was a knock on the door and the girl scampered over to answer it. Kensy's eyes were glued to the trio down below. She couldn't believe anyone would entrust them to clear the money. They probably kept it for themselves.

Max and Carlos hurried into the room. "We've got it!" Max waved a tired-looking piece of paper in his hand. "We know what the code says!"

Kensy spun around. "Well, out with it," she demanded.

Max took in a deep breath. "Proof of life and then I will do as you ask."

Kensy's eyes widened. "What?"

"That sounds like a ransom," Autumn said, her brow furrowing.

The boys nodded. "Our thoughts exactly," Carlos replied.

"Should we tell the teachers?" Kensy asked. "I mean, if the prime minister's son has been kidnapped, we can surely do something."

There was another knock at the door. Autumn answered it again and was surprised to see Miss Ziegler.

"Do you know where Max and Carlos are?" the teacher asked. "I was waking everyone up as we need to be on our way to the train by six-thirty and their room was empty."

Autumn opened the door wider. "They're here. They only just came up, but we need to tell you something."

Lottie walked into the room. One side was immaculate while the other looked like an explosion in a clothing factory. She didn't have to think too hard to work out which of the girls the mess belonged to. "Good morning," she said, eyeing the group warily. "You know you boys shouldn't be up here. Mr. Reffell might have a heart attack if he knew girls and boys were in each other's rooms – even if two of you are brother and sister."

She spotted the piece of paper on the end of the bed. "What's this?" She picked it up and studied the markings. "Good grief, this is a pigpen cipher. Where did you get it?"

And with that the children launched into the story of everything that had happened the past afternoon and where that note had come from.

Lottie Ziegler twisted a stray curl around her finger. "We need to call it in and see if there's any intel on Nico. But you do realize that, if there's nothing, we have no role to play. We can't go around getting involved in matters that are none of our business."

"But Nico's been kidnapped," Kensy said, appalled by the woman's indifference. "We saw his mother – she was praying and crying. She lied to a priest!"

"You don't know that for sure – there were photographs of the reunited family on the front page of the newspapers. There was even something in yesterday's *Beacon* – I read it myself," Lottie countered.

"What if that picture was old?" Carlos said. "They could have supplied it to the press to make them think he was back."

"That's true," Max said. "Maybe we can find a copy of one of the local rags downstairs."

"I don't think you should get too worked up." Lottie walked to the window and looked down into the piazza. "It might be something else entirely. The woman has quite a few troubles at the moment and Italian politics have always been tricky. Trust me. I'll see what I can find out, but if there's nothing, I suggest you forget about it and enjoy the rest of the trip."

Max sat down on the end of Autumn's bed. "I was kind of hoping we'd get to test our skills on a proper mission."

"Me too." Kensy couldn't help feeling a little miffed that, when she'd said as much on Christmas Day, her brother had sided with her grandmother against her.

Lottie looked at the lad and smiled kindly. "I know you're keen, Max, but believe me when I say you're not ready yet. And when you do find yourself in the middle of something, sometimes you'll wish you hadn't. Our line of business isn't exactly straightforward. Carlos and Autumn have been training for years and they haven't had a lot of field action, apart from rescuing you two in London, but one day, when you least expect it, everything you've learned will come in very handy. Now, hurry up and get dressed. It's almost six and you need to have some breakfast. The fast train to Naples leaves at seven-thirty and Mr. Reffell wants us out the door in half an hour."

* * *

Max placed the newspaper on the table. Miss Ziegler had handed it over as they'd hopped

259

aboard the train. The journey from Rome would take just over an hour, then they'd catch a local service from Naples to Pompeii. Max, along with Carlos, Autumn and Kensy, studied the picture of the prime minister and her husband and son. It appeared to have been taken on a balcony at the Palazzo Chigi and in the background they could see the Christmas tree and a glimpse of the protestors too.

"So much for that theory," Max said with a sigh.

Kensy's forehead was fixed in a permanent furrow. She realized she'd been so caught up in thinking about the prime minister for the past fourteen hours that she'd forgotten about her parents. A sharp stab of guilt hit her in the chest. What if, with all that distraction, she and Max had missed something important? As Max looked across at her, his mouth set in a grim line, she wondered if he could read her mind.

In the group of four seats across the aisle, Misha and Lola were doing their best to ignore Alfie and Graham. Graham was reading a book on space travel and Alfie had a rugby magazine open. Lola was harping on about her previous evening's purchases.

Kensy glanced across at Misha, who crossed her eyes in boredom. Lola caught sight of Kensy's attentions and sneered. "What are you staring at?" the girl said loudly.

Kensy shook her head. "Nothing."

"You were watching me, weren't you? You're always watching me." Lola made a face and sniggered.

"No, I'm not," Kensy said crossly.

Sensing trouble, Max tried to shoot his sister a warning look, but she refused to meet his eye.

"Yes, you are. You're doing it now." Lola pretended to shiver and looped arms with Misha. "It's so creepy."

Kensy rolled her eyes at Autumn, who twisted her mouth to stop herself from giggling. "Lola, I can assure you that I am not watching you and I don't want to be you and I don't think you're the most mesmerizing girl on earth," she said as nicely as she could.

Lola's eyes narrowed. "Did you just call me ugly?" Her bottom lip began to tremble. "Misha, say something!"

"Stop being mean to her," Misha blurted, although, for the first time since Kensy had known the girl, her words were a little less than convincing and Lola must have felt it too.

Lola's head swiveled sharply. "Whose side are you on?"

"Yours, of course," Misha replied. She turned to Kensy and shouted, "Leave her alone!"

"Okay." Kensy raised her palms in surrender, then glowered out the window.

Max couldn't shake the feeling that something was up with Misha. The girl seemed to have the weight of the world on her shoulders. He'd have to talk to her later, presuming they could get a minute alone without Lola lingering like a bad smell. "I'm going to get a drink," he said, standing up. "Does anyone want anything?"

"I'll come," Kensy volunteered. She hoped no one else joined them as she really wanted to speak to Max alone. Autumn asked her to bring back a bottle of water.

"I think I saw Dad," Max said quietly, once the pair had entered the next car.

"What?!" Kensy exploded, garnering glares from anyone within fifty paces. "When?"

"Keep it down," Max hissed.

"Why didn't you tell me?" Kensy demanded. "I can't believe you kept that to yourself."

"It was when those guys were chasing us yesterday, but then he disappeared into the crowd and I couldn't see him anymore," Max explained. "Maybe it wasn't even him. Maybe I just imagined it."

Kensy could hear the pain in her brother's voice. She knew she should give him a hug or show some sort of kindness, but she was still mad that he hadn't told her sooner. "I can't stand all this waiting. What could they possibly be doing for this long?"

Max nodded. "I've been thinking that the only thing that would be keeping them away from us is family."

Kensy looked at him in a way that suggested he had a screw loose. "But *we're* their family, and Granny and Fitz and Mim."

"And Mum's parents," Max said. He stopped and looked his sister in the eye. "What if they aren't dead – have you thought about that? What if they're the reason Mum and Dad and Fitz disappeared in the first place?"

Kensy thought for a moment. It made a strange sort of sense.

"There's a computer in the business center at the hotel. Tonight, when everyone's in bed, let's see what else we can find out about them," Max said.

Kensy reached out and pressed the button to enter the dining car. "Meet you there at midnight."

CHAPTER 26

⌐⊔◻⊔

Monty Reffell closed his eyes and leaned back in his seat. The day had been a huge success and he had reveled in the children's constant exclamations. Now he was going to allow himself a nap on the homeward journey. He nodded off, thinking that Pompeii was indeed one of the most interesting places on earth. It was so well preserved – even if the sight of all those plaster casts of dead bodies was a rather solemn reminder that the time capsule only existed because of the eruption of Mount Vesuvius and the destruction of everything around it.

"It must have been terrifying when the volcano exploded," Harper commented to Yasmina. "Knowing that they couldn't outrun it."

Yasmina nodded. "It reminds you of the power of Mother Nature – we're so small and insignificant in the whole scheme of things."

Sachin yawned. "It reminds me that I need to do something important with my life."

"What? Like becoming a scientist so you can find cures for terrible diseases?" Yasmina teased.

Max looked up from across the aisle. Her comment made him think of his grandparents and the sort of work they had done. Hopefully he and Kensy would be able to find out something more about them tonight.

"No, like playing cricket for England and making sure that we beat Australia in the Ashes," the boy replied, grinning.

The train rocketed through the countryside, slowing down only as they entered the larger towns along the route. Max had noticed several makeshift camps and banners, confirming that the food crisis was even worse outside of Rome. It was obvious the whole country was suffering.

Kensy and Autumn were playing their twelfth game of tic-tac-toe when Kensy suddenly realized what it was that had been bothering her the past couple of days. She held her pen aloft and looked at her brother. "Max, do you still have that newspaper?"

"Why?" he asked, and rummaged around in his daypack to find it.

"I don't think that boy in the picture is Nico," Kensy said.

The others looked at her as though she had lost her mind.

Autumn wrinkled her nose. "Why would the prime minister and her husband take a photo with a boy who's not their child? What could they possibly gain from doing that?"

Max laid the paper on the table and Kensy spun it around. The boy's face was partly obscured, but the mark behind his ear was clear as day. She dropped her voice to a whisper. "He's from the orphanage, I swear. I waved at him when they were all walking to the church and then I saw him near the Spanish Steps. I didn't realize it was the same kid until now."

"It's not the best photo, is it?" Carlos admitted.

"The boy from the orphanage has a mark behind his ear – just like that one," Kensy said, tapping the photo.

The skeptic in Max was unconvinced. "It could be a smudge from the ink, Kens."

"Let me see that." Carlos picked up the paper and examined it.

"Think about it," Kensy insisted. "Whoever has Nico sent another boy who looks like him to have his picture taken with the family so everyone thinks he's gone home. But now they're blackmailing the prime minister. That kid there is the key to everything."

"The Italian secret service must be on it," Carlos said.

Kensy raised an eyebrow at the boy. "If there was the possibility that your child's life was in danger, would you tell anyone?"

The others couldn't deny she had a point.

As the train pulled into the Roma Termini, Mr. Reffell was jolted awake by Mrs. Vanden Boom barking orders at everyone to gather their things. The children assembled on the crowded platform with the teachers.

"We need to find that kid," Kensy hissed, pulling on her daypack. "And I'm pretty sure I know exactly where he'll be."

That was the end of their conversation as the teachers rounded up their groups before setting off.

"Do we really have to walk again?" Lola whined.

Romilly Vanden Boom nodded. If only she had a pound for every time that child complained about something she'd have been able to treat them all to a fancy meal. "It's not far."

"But my feet hurt," the girl moaned, and was swiftly joined by Misha grumbling too.

"We're stopping for dinner on the way back," Mr. Reffell said. He'd been pleased to have secured a lovely little trattoria near Quirinal Palace and had prepaid for the meal before they left England. It was slightly off the beaten track and apparently much loved by locals, which is precisely what he wanted.

The children dodged their way through the evening commuters, doing their best to stay within close proximity of their group leaders. Once they were on the street, it was clear that the protesters had spread to other parts of the city. People with placards were standing on just about every corner.

"Wow, is it really that bad?" Harper said. There were men and women of all ages, families with small children and even a group of priests, all chanting about the price of wheat.

"I'm afraid so. Rationing has started," Mr. Frizzle said, shaking his head. "It's a ghastly state of affairs."

As the group neared a supermarket, they realized there was a queue snaking out the door and around the corner.

"It's ridiculous." Inez shook her head. "We're in Italy. I could imagine something like this in the third world, but it's almost unthinkable here."

The restaurant they were heading to was tucked away in a quiet lane. Mr. Reffell had consulted the map several times, but was now checking his phone for good measure.

"Are you sure we're in the right place, sir?" Dante asked as they made their way down a long alley littered with scooters and garbage bins. Washing lines were slung above them and a black cat scuttled across their path. "This looks a bit dodgy, if you ask me."

Monty bit his lip. He'd been thinking the same thing. There wasn't a storefront in sight and the lighting was terribly poor. "Wait here while I go on and check," he said, and gratefully accepted Max's offer to accompany him. He was confident the boy's photographic memory would see them in the right place in no time.

They hadn't walked much further when Max spied a tiny sign with an arrow pointing toward a gate. Monty pressed the buzzer and was admitted into a narrow passageway. At the end was a door and the sound of people laughing on the other side.

"Thank heavens for that," the teacher said, and sent Max to beckon the others.

Inside, the decor was quintessentially Italian with red-checked tablecloths and chianti bottles turned into candleholders. Plastic grapevines covered the ceiling and walls, and the bar area was crowded with rowdy patrons. They were greeted by a waiter with a thick black moustache, who ushered the group through a set of double doors into a private room.

"Well, isn't this charming?" Monty said with an appreciative nod. He was feeling very pleased with himself and made a note to thank his friend for the recommendation.

The children were quickly seated at two large round tables. Soon after, the waiter returned with bread baskets and little dishes of olive oil. There was certainly no sign of the wheat shortage in this restaurant. Monty was relieved he'd already paid too, as he spotted a menu and almost choked at the prices.

Max and Carlos excused themselves for the bathroom, racing up the back stairs until a loud bang stopped them in their tracks.

It sounded like a hand hitting a tabletop and it was accompanied by a definitive "No!" They looked around and found a window high up in the wall. Intrigued, they crept closer.

"*Lei firmerà i documenti*," a woman said hotly.

There was another loud thump.

"Speak *Inglese* – you know the waiters only speak *Italiano*."

"Fine," the woman hissed in heavily accented English. "She will sign the document tomorrow. Penina will be under our control after that and from then on *we* will set the food prices and govern the farmers. The people will be at our mercy. We will offer concessions at first to win their favor, then raise the prices over time. We will make a fortune."

"And what about the boy?" the man said.

Max and Carlos looked at one another.

"The trade will take place at the eastern end of the Piazza del Popolo," the woman replied. "You can watch from the roadway above and know that the deal is done. I still cannot believe he fell through the roof. We had been planning to snatch him the very next day."

"And if she doesn't sign the papers?" the man asked.

"We kill him," the woman said without a trace of emotion.

Carlos pointed at the window. He retrieved a nearby stool with a wobbly leg and was about to step up onto it when Max grabbed his arm.

"I'm taller," the boy mouthed. Carlos held the stool steady as Max stretched as far as he could. His fingers gripped the edge of the windowsill as he slowly hauled himself up. He peered into the room, his heart racing. There were three people seated at a round table. The decor was far fancier than downstairs and reminded him of his grandmother's small sitting room, which was full of antiques, with a sprinkling of Italian flavor.

"Can you see them?" Carlos whispered.

Max nodded. There was a large man facing away from him. He was bald on top with thick dark hair in a ring around the back of his head. His long sleeves were pushed up and Max could see a tattoo on the inside of his forearm.

It was the same script as the man from the street except this time Max could see that it said "Nero," not "hero." Opposite him was a man with gray hair who was smoking a cigar. A woman with long black hair and a made-up face was beside him. She was very pretty and had a movie-star look about her. Max's eyes widened when it dawned on him that he'd seen her before. He was almost certain she was the woman who had left the orphanage in the middle of the night and gotten behind the wheel of that black Ferrari in the piazza.

Two burly men were stationed on either side of the door. Max gasped when he recognized one of them as the fellow they'd seen inside the gates of Quirinal Palace with the gun holstered in his jacket. But if that was troubling, his heart almost leapt through his chest when he realized that the other guard was one of the thugs who had been chasing them in the street yesterday.

Carlos desperately wanted to see too. He let go of Max's stool to look for something else to climb onto. Max wobbled unsteadily and, feeling his feet give way from under him, grabbed onto the windowsill. The stool clattered onto the tiles.

"What was that?" the large man bellowed.

Max thought fast and jumped to the ground. He returned the stool to its original position and joined Carlos just as a door opened at the end of the passageway and a face appeared. It was the man from the palace. Max thanked their lucky stars it wasn't the other guy. He would have recognized them in an instant.

Max looked at Carlos, a confused expression on his face. Carlos glanced around as if he were lost. "*Toilette?*" Max said in his best Italian accent.

The man grunted and pointed down the hallway.

"*Grazie.*" The boys nodded and hurried off, not daring to say another word in case they gave themselves away. When they walked back into the hall, the man was still there, watching them like a hawk.

"*Grazie,*" Max said again as he and Carlos sped past.

"What took you so long?" Kensy asked as

they sat down. "I thought you'd fallen in."

"Tell you later," Max replied, feeling a little rattled by the encounter.

Kensy eyed him and Carlos warily. "Tell me *now*," she insisted.

Max took a piece of pepperoni pizza and put it on his plate. "Let's just say that maybe your hunch about Nico is correct, and if that's the case, I don't think any of us will be getting much sleep tonight."

CHAPTER 27

⌑◰⎅⎁⎅◁⎐⎏⎚⎍◁⌁

"Finally," Kensy muttered, as their hotel came into view. They'd barely had a second alone since leaving the restaurant as it seemed everyone wanted to chat. In snatches here and there, Max had relayed the gist of what he and Carlos had encountered at the restaurant.

"So, you think the guy who was watching you was one of the president's bodyguards?" Autumn said.

"Well, I don't know for sure, but Carlos and I saw him when we were passing Quirinal Palace the other day. He had a Glock pistol inside a shoulder holster, so we presumed he was protecting the president."

The children hadn't noticed that Misha was right behind them. She had one ear on their conversation while trying to filter Lola's moaning about her sore feet. Fed up, she turned to the girl, a ripple of anger pulsing through her. "Seriously, Lola, could you just give up your whining for one minute?"

A stunned silence followed as everyone stopped in their tracks to look at her, their mouths agape. Lola couldn't have been more shocked if she'd sat on an electric fence.

"*What* did you say?" she asked.

"You heard me," Misha said. Her face flushed and her hands formed two small fists by her sides. "All you do is complain when, really, you've got nothing to complain about. You're spoiled and ridiculous and I've had enough!"

Romilly Vanden Boom blinked in surprise. It was impossible to tell whether this was part of a larger plan or if Misha was actually sick and tired of the brat. She couldn't have blamed her for the latter.

"What's the matter with you?" Lola snapped, her eyebrows forming a sharp "V." "I–I'm your best friend. I'm your *only* friend because, let's face it, you're a loser!"

With a cry of exasperation, Misha stalked off without so much as a backward glance.

"You can forget about us sharing a room!" Lola screeched, stamping her foot. "Sleep in the fountain for all I care! I hate you!"

"Mission accomplished," Misha muttered, and was soon joined by Autumn and Kensy.

"You okay?" Autumn asked, her face a picture of concern.

Misha nodded. "Just look like you're worried about me and we'll talk back at the hotel."

Kensy gave the girl a sly wink and giggled. "Bet that felt good."

Fortunately, the hotel was a hop, skip and a jump away.

"I'll get my things and bunk with Autumn and Kensy, if that's okay with you," Misha said to Miss Ziegler as they stepped into the foyer.

Lola's eyes bulged as if her head were about to explode. "Why would you want to be *their* friend?" she demanded. "They're horrible and stinky and . . . and they have silly names!"

Misha considered the girl as one might consider a blood-sucking mollusk. "Perhaps if you stopped to think about who's really the horrible one, you'd realize that most of the time it's you. I'm not your puppet or your slave anymore, Lola," she said calmly, then turned to walk up the stairs.

"Right, I think it's time for bed," Mrs. Vanden Boom said, clasping her hands tightly. "Off to have your showers and then it's lights-out in fifteen minutes. It's been a very long day and I'm sure we could all do with a rest. Good night, everyone."

Not five minutes later, Misha had been installed with Kensy and Autumn.

"So what was that about?" Autumn said. "You know you'll have to apologize and then she's going to hate us even more."

Misha shook her head. "Perhaps it won't come to that. I needed some time alone with you guys after what I overheard Max saying about the bodyguard from the palace.

I'd hazard that man isn't the president's security detail but Sergio Leonardi's."

Kensy and Autumn shot her confused looks. "Lola's father?" Kensy said.

Misha nodded. "One and the same. He also goes by Steve Lemmler back in London. I was surprised when Lola said that her parents were here in Italy, but I was absolutely stunned to see her father at Quirinal Palace the other day when we were walking back from the Colosseum. I don't know if she saw him too, but, if she did, she isn't saying anything."

It didn't take long for Max and Carlos to appear. They knocked quietly and Kensy let them in. The children sat facing each other on the two single beds.

"I thought you were up to something," Max said to Misha. "I saw the exasperation in your eyes earlier in the day."

Misha sighed. "I just had to get away from Lola. She's like a leech and . . . Well, enough of that. I need you to go over everything. Who were the people you saw and what were they talking about?"

Max recounted what he'd told Kensy and Autumn, and added that he thought he'd seen the woman before.

Kensy hopped up and walked to the window. "I saw her too!" she said excitedly. "I thought it was a strange picture, really – the fancy car and the orphanage . . . But now we know what those kids get up to, maybe it's not so strange after all."

Misha frowned. "The man with the terrible hair and the big nose is definitely Sergio Leonardi and the other man is Nero Rinaldi, the president of Italy. I don't know about the woman."

"Nero . . . Lola's father has that name tattooed on his forearm and I think the thug who chased us yesterday has it on his wrist," Max pondered aloud.

Autumn quickly filled Misha in on how they'd been pursued by three men after stumbling upon them using the children as pickpockets. "Is the Italian president a friend of Lola's father?" Autumn asked her.

"We think they belong to the same organization," Misha said. "We know that Sergio has his dirty fingers in lots of different pies, but we've never been able to pin anything significant on him. He's as slick as Teflon and has a boatload of shelf companies and aliases. He's never been caught for anything, but I feel as though we're close. Intel says he's been working on an arms deal with the Middle East, but there's no trail."

"So they're Mafia?" Carlos said.

Misha shook her head. "Diavolo. They're like a myth, though. No one has ever been able to prove their existence and I suspect they want to keep it that way."

"Diavolo means 'devil' in Italian," Kensy said. "Are they worse than the Mafia?"

Misha nodded. "They're the worst of the worst – from some of the things I've read, they're the most evil group in the world and also the most difficult to trace."

"Do you think the tattoo means something?" Autumn asked. "Why Nero? He was a Roman emperor with a very bad reputation – is it possible that he started the Diavolo?"

Misha shrugged apologetically. "That I don't know."

"Who can stop them then?" Kensy asked. "I mean, if the president is part of the group, he clearly considers himself above the law. Never mind how many other officials are in his pocket. What if the corruption goes all the way to the police commissioner?"

Misha bit down on her thumbnail. "We trust no one other than a man called Alessandro Grimaldi. He's head of the Italian secret service with links to Pharos. Your grandmother thinks he's the only one who can help bring them down."

Max scratched his head and thought for a moment. "What if it's not arms they're dealing?"

The others looked at him.

"What if it's wheat and pasta? The woman said that, when the prime minister signs the papers, they'll be in control of Penina. I thought they were talking about a place, but isn't that the biggest pasta company in Italy? What if they're blackmailing the prime minister to hand over control of the food?

I bet Sergio's gang are behind the crop failures too. They've been driving up the prices so the prime minister would be left with no choice and now they have her son as the ultimate bargaining chip."

"Wow, Max, that's a pretty amazing theory," Autumn said admiringly.

Carlos looked at Misha. "Could it be true?"

"Anything's possible," the girl replied. "I contacted Dame Spencer to tell her what I'd seen, but there aren't any agents available – whatever else is happening is taking up loads of resources. It's just us. She said I had her blessing to mobilize if things here escalated."

"So, we're on a real mission?" Kensy said, her eyes lighting up.

Misha nodded solemnly. "We have a maximum of eleven agents-in-training and four dormant field agents at our disposal – but we have to make sure that the other kids are kept out of the way. We can't blow our cover."

Kensy felt a ripple of anticipation course through her body. "We have to find Nico before his mother signs those documents." She gasped as an idea came to her. "If we locate that other boy first, he can lead us to him." She jumped to her feet. "Come on, what are we waiting for?"

"Kens, we need a strategy," Max said. "There's no point running around the city aimlessly. What if Nico's –"

"Right under our noses," Autumn said, looking across the piazza at the orphanage. "That place is full of children and that boy from the photograph is bound to be there. We know he's one of the gang . . . Would anyone notice an extra? And Miss Ziegler said that Nico ran away across the rooftops. He could have easily ended up there by chance – just like you heard that woman say. It's not that mad an idea when you think about it . . ."

Kensy sat down on the edge of the bed and groaned. "Fine, party poopers, but I still think we've got to get out there tonight – before it's too late."

On that they all agreed.

CHAPTER 28

Carlos kept watch on the orphanage while they brainstormed their plans. Luckily, he'd thought to bring his special reading glasses – which were actually thermal binoculars – and used them to work out a rough map of the building.

"I think the children are on the fourth floor," he said, raising the glasses to the top of his head. "There's more concentrated heat there than anywhere else."

"What about the basement or the attic?" Max asked. "They're the most obvious places to hold someone captive. I doubt they'd keep Nico with the other kids – he'd be more likely to escape that way."

Carlos put on his glasses again and had a look, but there didn't seem to be anything bigger than a mouse in either of those places.

"How are we going to get in?" Autumn asked.

Carlos had already worked that out. He'd spotted an old coal chute up against the building that would give them direct access to the cellar. It was shielded from the piazza by a road work sign, but there was a padlock.

"We can't all go," he said. "If something happens, we'll need at least two of us to launch a rescue mission – and perhaps it should be me and Autumn. We've had a bit of experience in that department."

Max grinned, recalling how Carlos and Autumn had come to his and Kensy's aid in London, when a couple of brutes had tried to kidnap them off the street.

While the children were busy planning, Misha had gone to tell Miss Ziegler what was going on, but the woman wasn't in her room. Misha then tried the other teachers, but none of them were about either. The only rational explanation was that they were all working on something for the main mission and were meeting somewhere in secret. At this point, it looked as though they were going it alone. She thought about involving the other kids but decided to keep things low-key, at least until they worked out if Nico was actually in the orphanage. Too many trainee agents on a real mission could easily get out of hand.

"If we're not back in an hour, you know what to do," Max said. Carlos threw him his black beanie and Kensy pulled a sweater over her head.

"Should we test comms again?" Kensy asked. She'd given Autumn her watch so that they could communicate through Max's.

The last time Mrs. Vanden Boom had examined it, she'd found a radio transmitter and a tiny earpiece that you could pull out from the dial. In fact, the woman had studied the watches on several occasions now and each time had discovered another fascinating feature.

Autumn gave Kensy a hug. "Good luck."

Max leaned in for one too, which set Autumn's heart rate on double time. Carlos and Misha gave them a wave as they left the room. The trio watched from the window as the pair headed into the piazza, which was still crowded with tourists.

"There they are," Autumn said, spotting Kensy and Max below.

Max pretended to run his hand through his hair, positioning his watch by his mouth. "Can you hear me?" he asked.

"Loud and clear," Autumn replied, her eyes tracing Kensy's movements as the girl rounded the back of the road work sign. She saw Kensy take out her hair clip and, no more than ten seconds later, she and Max disappeared.

* * *

Kensy slid down the narrow chute and flicked on her tiny flashlight to illuminate the dingy space. Apart from a few lumps of coal in the corner, the room was stacked with pallets of beer and cigarettes. There was another tower of boxes containing olive oil and several sacks of onions, some of which must have already gone bad, given the stench.

Max put on Carlos's heat-seeking glasses as Kensy listened at the door. Once he gave her the signal, she pulled it open and checked the hallway with a small pocket mirror. "It's clear," she whispered, and ventured outside.

The air was thick with damp as the twins crept to the end of the hallway. Max pointed up a set of wooden stairs and Kensy stepped onto the bottom tread, wincing as it groaned under her weight. The second step creaked too. Max followed behind her, holding his breath until they reached a small landing. The pair of them crept to a door with a circular glass panel in the top half and froze when they heard voices on the other side. Max had made the rookie error of not using Carlos's glasses to check if anyone was there.

After a moment's pause, Kensy stood on her tiptoes and peered through the porthole into a large kitchen. There was an ancient stove and a long table littered with beer bottles and abandoned dinner plates. Seated around it were the three men who had chased them and the older fellow who they'd seen collecting the stolen items from the children. There was another man in a pinstriped suit with his back to them.

A woman entered the room from a side door. It was Sister Maria Regina. Although dressed in her habit, she was without her wimple. Her long dark hair floated about her shoulders, but it was what she did next that made Kensy gasp in horror. The woman gripped one side of her face, gouging her skin. With a sharp tug, her entire visage came away. Her face was instantly transformed from the middle-aged nun with the huge nose into the young woman who Kensy had seen leaving the orphanage the other night. She then removed her teeth too and put them in a jar by the sink.

Kensy gagged and looked away. "*Eww.* Now, that's where I draw the line."

"What's the matter?" Max said impatiently. He didn't think it was a good idea for both

of them to be peering through the window –
they were more likely to be seen.

"It's the woman," Kensy whispered. She
turned back in time to see Sister Maria Regina
tousle her hair and spotted a mark – no, a
word – behind her ear. Nero.

"Sister Maria Regina is Diavolo too," Kensy
said out of the corner of her mouth. "She's
been wearing a mask this entire time – and it's
gross. Be grateful you didn't have to see it for
yourself. Talk about taking one for the team."
The girl's mind suddenly turned to Shugs. Was
that how he'd fooled everyone – with a mask?
But there was no time to worry about him
now. She'd have to mull over that one later.

Unable to resist, Max popped up beside
her to steal a peek. He immediately recognized
Sister Maria Regina as the woman in the
restaurant.

The twins surveyed the rest of the group
and noticed that they all had the same word
inked on their wrists. The man in the suit stood
up and walked to the other end of the room.
Kensy felt a stab of disappointment when she

realized he was the fellow who she'd thought had his wallet stolen near the Spanish Steps. Her hunch that he and the boy had been up to something had been right. For now she and Max weren't going any further – not in this direction, anyway.

"*Ho vinto!*" The older man slapped his hand of cards onto the table and laughed uproariously. He rose to his feet, scraping his chair against the floorboards, then spooned indeterminate food onto a plate and made his way straight toward the twins. They ducked their heads and scrambled back down the stairs, along the passage and into the storeroom. Seconds later, heavy footsteps thumped in the hallway.

"Nico must be down here somewhere," Max whispered. "He's bringing food."

"Or they've run out of beer." Kensy gulped, realizing they were definitely hiding in the wrong room if that were the case.

The pair listened at the door then pulled it open ever so slightly. They could see the older fellow pause at the room diagonally across from them. He banged on the door and yelled something in Italian. When there was no reply, he opened a small box in the wall and was about to place the plate of food in it when he must have caught sight of something. The plate smashed onto the floor as he turned the key in the lock. He charged into the room and caused an almighty ruckus before racing out and up the stairs, shouting at the top of his lungs.

The twins closed the door and turned to one another. Kensy's heart was pounding a million miles a minute. Although her Italian wasn't the best, she thought she had a fair idea of what the man had said . . . but how was it possible?

Max, his face ashen, raised his watch to his lips. "We're too late. He's gone."

CHAPTER 29

DELJED
BCAPe

Kensy was about to climb up the chute when a sound came from near the pallet of boxes. She paused and pressed a finger to her lips, then gestured toward them. It might have only been a rat, but she had to know for sure.

Max frowned then, cottoning on, joined her in tiptoeing toward the stack. They split up, each taking one side, all the while listening out for the men in the corridor. No doubt they were going to burst in any minute now. Just as Kensy peered around the corner, a boy covered from head to toe in grime ran at her, knocking her out of the way.

"Stop!" she cried, hitting the floor.

As the lad scurried up the chute, Max grabbed him around the ankles and held fast. "Nico, we're here to help you," he explained in broken Italian. "Please – you need to come with us. Your mother is in danger and you are too."

The boy struggled to break free but stopped once Max's words had registered. His chest heaved as his eyes, wide with fear, darted back and forth between Max and his sister.

"You have to believe us," Max pleaded. "They'll kill you otherwise."

Nico's eyes were wild, like an animal caught in a trap, but something Max had said must have worked because his body relaxed and he nodded.

Slowly, Max let go and introduced himself. "That's my sister, Kensy," he added with a smile, "and we're going to get you out of here."

They could hear yelling in the corridor and the sound of pounding footsteps and crashing doors.

"We've got to go," Kensy said. She raced

ahead of the boys and shoved the hatch, hoping that the piazza was still crowded.

Nico followed after her with Max bringing up the rear. He pulled his feet through the chute as the storeroom door flew open. Max closed the hatch and secured the padlock just as someone bashed against it from the other side.

Kensy turned to Nico and placed a hand on his shoulder. "You have to come with us. The only way we're going to catch those guys is if you do as we ask."

Nico shivered then nodded his head again.

Taking his hand in hers, Kensy led the way across the piazza and into the hotel at break-neck speed. Moments later, the trio were safe and sound in Autumn and Kensy's room. Nico sat on the end of Kensy's bed, a mixture of terror, confusion and relief on his face.

"You'll be safe here for now," Max said to the boy in Italian.

"Shall I get some food?" Autumn asked, wondering what one was supposed to offer a recently rescued hostage. "I'm sure I can find something in the kitchen."

"I'll help you," Misha offered.

"I am not hungry," Nico replied in English, to the group's surprise. "But perhaps later I may have a shower?"

"Oh, he speaks," Kensy noted wryly. "And in our mother tongue."

Nico managed a shy smile and shrugged. "I study English at school."

This was going to make things a lot easier for everyone.

"Please, you must tell me who are you and why were you looking for me?" Nico asked. His eyes scanned each one of their faces in bewilderment.

It was hard to know where to start, but between the five of them, they filled Nico in on all the details and why it was crucial that he stayed with them until they worked out their plan of attack. Given the president and Diavolo were involved, there was far too much at stake to return him to his mother just yet.

"And I think I've worked out the significance of Nero," Misha said. While the twins had ventured behind enemy lines, she had taken herself to the business center to do some research. "Well, we all know the ancient ruler was an evil man. The Diavolo have used his name as their symbol. It turns out that the letters of Nero Caesar represented by numbers in Hebrew add up to 666 – the number of the devil. It's actually not that clever because there's heaps of information about it on the internet."

Nico shook his head. "I cannot believe I was unlucky enough to have fallen through the roof of that awful place. They must have thought I was the best Christmas gift ever."

"If it makes you feel any better, they were planning to kidnap you anyway," Max said.

Kensy spun around on a chair by the desk. "Where were you going that night?" she asked the boy.

"I was running away to be with my grandfather. He and my mother don't get along anymore and I miss him so much. He was cruel to my mother when she remarried. I have been horrible to her too. My mother was a lawyer, but she had higher ambitions and wanted to help everyone. I blamed my stepfather for encouraging her into politics. She was so loved to begin with, but now the people hate her and she has made terrible mistakes. I have not made life any easier for her or my stepfather. He has tried so hard with me, but all I have done is push him away." Tears welled in the boy's eyes. It was the first time he'd allowed himself to cry. He just wished it wasn't happening now in front of three girls.

Kensy fetched him tissues from the bathroom and saved one for herself. She hadn't thought about her own parents since the train trip, and at the mention of Nico's mother, she'd felt a stab of despair like a punch in the stomach. There hadn't been time to try to find out more about their grandparents either.

Max looked at her and tugged on his left earlobe – it was their secret way of saying things would be all right. She didn't even want to think otherwise.

CHAPTER 30

THETRAP

"Who exactly are you?" Nico looked at Elliot Frizzle, who, along with Lottie Ziegler and the girls, were now crammed into Max and Carlos's hotel room. Shards of light pierced the room through the edges of the drawn curtains and a cacophony of bells tolled across the waking city.

Kensy had perched herself on the end of Max's bed while Autumn sat at the writing desk, and Misha had found herself a spot on the toilet seat, which faced straight into the bedroom. The teachers stood on either side of the door, looking a picture of bemusement.

"I'm an art teacher and Miss Ziegler's a math teacher and, together with the students, we're on a history tour of Rome," Elliot replied. "Although it doesn't quite feel like it at the moment."

"No, I mean . . . *who* are you really?" Nico repeated. "I do not understand why a group of English children would try to rescue me and how they would even know my mamma was being blackmailed."

Elliot leaned against the doorjamb and folded his arms. "I'm afraid that's rather by the by. All you need to know, Nico, is that you can trust us and we will do everything in our power to get you back home safely."

"Do you really think we can pull it off, sir?" Max asked. His mind had been running over everything they'd learned about the Diavolo in the past twelve hours, twisting and turning the information like a Rubik's cube. Catching them was going to be tricky but incredibly exhilarating at the same time.

"I have every faith," Elliot said with a nod.

Nico had slept soundly for the first time since he'd run away on Christmas Eve. Carlos had given up his bed to the boy and had shared with Max. The pair of them had been awake half the night, partly keeping an eye on their guest to make sure that he didn't try to leave, and mostly thinking about the plan to bring down the Diavolo, which they had plotted out with their teachers overnight.

"Alessandro Grimaldi will have agents stationed on every corner. You'll be watched, but you're going to have to keep one step ahead of them all the way," Lottie said. "If the men from the orphanage suspect foul play, it will jeopardize everything."

Nico's head snapped up. "Who is Alessandro Grimaldi?" he asked. "I have heard that name before."

"Someone who can stop the people who have been blackmailing your mother," Elliot Frizzle said. "Now, let's organize some breakfast while we wait for the others to leave for the day. Miss Ziegler is going to shadow you once you're out on the street. Mrs. Vanden

Boom and I will accompany the rest of the children to the church this morning with Mr. Reffell. He's organized a tour. It's going to be very interesting, actually. Apparently, the hearts and internal organs of over thirty popes are embalmed and stored in urns over there – absolutely fascinating stuff – and then we're off to the Villa Borghese gardens."

Kensy blanched. "What?! I intercepted the prime minister's note in one of the urns in that church – gross! What if I was touching the heart of a pope?"

Autumn chuckled and Max grinned to himself.

"I'd consider it an honor – perhaps even a blessing," Elliot said, a smile twitching at the corners of his mouth.

"What are you going to tell the others?" Carlos asked. He couldn't imagine they would be able to disappear for the day without causing some discussion among the rest of the group.

Elliot Frizzle scratched his head. "You've all come down with a stomach bug and we're keeping you in isolation – Miss Ziegler drew the short straw and has to look after you."

That sounded feasible enough. Even the other agents-in-training wouldn't question that and, when it came down to it, no one wanted a case of the vomits. But if they were needed at all, the adults had already decided that Elliot would look after the five students who weren't part of Pharos – which the man really did consider as drawing the short straw; he would have loved to see some active duty himself.

Carlos gazed at the piazza. He spotted one of the men from the orphanage running and speaking into his sleeve. They must have been frantic, wondering where Nico was, but soon enough he would reappear and things would be turned completely upside down.

* * *

Mrs. Vanden Boom had the children out the door at nine o'clock, heading for the Santi Vincenzo e Anastasio a Trevi church on the corner. They would only be there half an hour or so before they set off for the gardens, so it was decided that the others would stay put and keep watch on the orphanage until then.

As to be expected, Lola was still blisteringly angry with Misha and thought it served the girl right to come down with gastro after she'd ditched her for Autumn and Kensington. Lola attached herself to Hattie, who was a sympathetic ear, given she was prone to the odd angry outburst herself and found it difficult to make friends.

"Why can I not go home?" Nico asked. He'd been thinking about his mother and stepfather and how worried they would be. "Does my mamma know I have escaped?"

Lottie Ziegler shook her head. "No, we need her to believe you're still being held so she'll agree to sign the papers and make the exchange. We have to get our timing just right – and that's why we need you to lead them on a wild-goose chase until then. We have sent a message to your mother, which she will think is from the kidnappers, and we have sent the kidnappers a message from her about the exchange. Of course, each has been fed a different story. The Diavolo think they are going to meet her at the Piazza del Popolo at half past eleven, but we need you to lead them to Quirinal Palace at half past ten."

"All right, shall we go over things one more time?" Max said, spreading out the map of the city on the bed. The others gathered around. "First, we need to make it known to the thugs at the orphanage that you are close by – and that all starts here." He jabbed a finger at the picture of the Trevi Fountain. "Then we will lead them on the chase of a lifetime."

"And don't worry," Kensy said to Nico. "Max has a photographic memory. He won't let us get lost and we've already outrun them once before."

"I am not worried about that. I have some skills of my own," Nico said with a grin.

The briefing continued for another twenty minutes until Miss Ziegler, who had stationed herself by the window, saw Mrs. Vanden Boom leading the children across the piazza with Mr. Frizzle and Mr. Reffell bringing up the rear. Once she received the signal from Romilly, Lottie turned to the children. "It's time."

CHAPTER 31

J JrELWFOOᴇ
a DiSCOVERY

The man in the suit stubbed out his cigarette in an overflowing ashtray and sat back with a sigh. After a sleepless night, he was sporting a five o'clock shadow and dark circles under his eyes. Some days he wondered if he should retire to the countryside and live a quiet life, but he knew that he couldn't live without her and she would never agree to move away from the city.

"From her latest communication," he began, "it is clear the boy has not returned home and she is expecting us to make the drop this morning, as planned. But it is impossible to make the exchange if we do not have the goods."

"How did the boy escape in the first place, Giovanni? Hmm?" Sister Maria Regina inspected her manicured nails and glowered at the other man at the end of the table. "I thought we had the entire building under surveillance."

Giovanni cradled his head in his hands and swallowed hard. He had forgotten that fact last night. Perhaps his old age was catching up to him.

The woman looked up, as if reading his mind. "Do you mean to tell me you have not checked?" she hissed. Taking his silence as confirmation, she slammed her hand on the tabletop, rattling the glasses. "Well, don't just sit there – check the footage now! I want to know exactly how he got out. And you –" She threw an old newspaper at one of two young men standing in the room. It had Nico's photo on the front, its edges beginning to curl. "Show his picture to the children and everyone else here and tell them to get out on the street and start searching. Or you will all be sent to work in the mill!"

Both men nodded and hurried away, followed by Giovanni.

"Why do I employ such imbeciles?" the woman muttered to herself. She pouted when she saw she'd broken a nail.

"Indeed," the man in the suit said, and took a sip of his coffee. "I presume you have visited the church this morning."

"Of course," she replied. "It is done."

Giovanni charged back through the door, jiggling about as if he needed the toilet.

The woman looked at him. "Out with it! What did you find?"

"He escaped through the hatch where we passed the food – the boy must be some kind of a contortionist," the man said, sounding impressed.

"You idiot!" she fumed, and threw the ashtray at him.

"Yes, yes," Giovanni said, ducking out of the way in time. The ashtray smashed into the wall behind him. "But that is not all. Two of the children who noticed our business transactions the other day were in the basement.

They helped the boy escape through the chute in the cellar."

The younger man, who had just returned to retrieve his jacket, gasped. "I know where they are!" he said. "I saw them in the piazza when I was speaking with the *poliziotti*. They are staying in the hotel across from the fountain."

"Find them and get the boy," Sister Maria Regina demanded, her lips quivering. "And when you do, make sure they are never seen again!"

CHAPTER 32

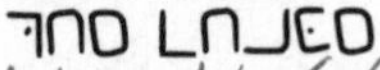

the chase

The children stood inside the hotel entrance. Lottie Ziegler's task was to shadow them. Carlos, Autumn and Misha would keep close too. Once Nico had the thugs' attention, he had to lead them to Quirinal Palace instead of the Piazza del Popolo, where they thought they were making the drop. So long as everything went to plan, his mother would be there waiting for him. It all depended on everyone receiving the right messages and leaving at the right times; Mr. Reffell had been busy in the church early this morning intercepting and replacing communications.

Lottie smiled at the children. "Good luck, everyone."

"You go ahead," Max said, nodding at Nico. "We'll be right behind you."

The boy opened the hotel door and stepped outside. The instant he did, a muscly arm grabbed him and a large hand covered his mouth to muffle his screams.

Nico bit down on the man's fingers with all his might. "Help!" he cried.

Max launched himself out the door and onto the man's back. The brute spun around and around, trying to shake him off, until Misha scissor kicked the fellow in the chin. Max jumped out of the way as the man crashed onto the pavement. Where there was one, there had to be more and, sure enough, two other men came running toward them. Carlos and Autumn created a diversion, ducking and weaving their way through the throng of tourists and across the piazza.

"Go!" Miss Ziegler called out. "I can deal with these two."

And that she did, punching one fellow on

the nose and cartwheeling the heel of her boot into the forehead of the other. They both groaned in pain as Misha gave them swift kicks to the ribs for good measure. Unfortunately, that wasn't enough to keep them down. Seconds later, they scraped themselves off the cobblestones and gave chase.

Although the piazza was already brimming with tourists, the *poliziotti* seemed to turn a completely blind eye, despite an elderly couple pointing in the children's direction and indicating to the officers there was something untoward going on.

The twins, meanwhile, sped after Nico. Kensy turned to see a man thundering behind them. "Hurry, he's gaining on us!" she panted. "And he's brought some friends with him for the ride. How rude."

Max snuck a look. "Those are the kids from the orphanage!"

But the man wasn't interested in the twins. He raced past them and was almost within reach of Nico.

"Look out!" Max yelled.

Nico grinned. Now was the fun part. Everyone watched on in amazement as he ran sideways up a wall and spun in the air, dodging the man's grasp. He landed in the middle of the roadway, several feet behind the fellow – right in the path of a speeding scooter. It skidded to a halt in front of the boy.

"Oh no, he's done for." Kensy winced, and almost fainted when the rider flipped his visor. "Fitz, what are you doing here?" she cried.

"Nico, get on." Fitz grabbed the boy and hurled him onto the seat behind him. "It's okay. I'm with them."

The other thugs were catching up, despite Autumn and Carlos's best attempts to thwart their progress. Fitz revved the engine and swung the scooter around one hundred and eighty degrees. The man up ahead hauled a young fellow from another scooter and almost crashed into a parked car as he took off after them.

"We need wheels," Kensy said, looking around. "We'll never keep up with them on foot."

"Do you mean to steal a car?" Max was

aghast at the thought and a little excited too.

Kensy rolled her eyes. "*Borrow*. We'll bring it back," she said, and ran along a row of parked vehicles, checking to see if any had keys in the ignition. Hot-wiring wasn't a skill she and Max had studied yet. But there was nothing. Just as they reached a T-intersection, a tiny Fiat flew past. It screeched to a stop and reversed wildly toward them. "Oh no, who's this guy?" Kensy groaned, changing course to avoid the car.

"Kensy! Max!" a voice shouted through the open window.

Max turned and squinted into the vehicle. "Uncle Rupert?"

"Thought you might need a hand," the man said. "Jump in!"

To their shock, Rupert scrambled into the back seat.

"What are you doing?" Max demanded, looking at his uncle as though he'd lost his mind.

"Well, I don't think it's the best idea to let you loose with one of these if I need to use it," Rupert replied, lifting a double-barreled shotgun from under the seat.

"Shove over," Kensy said to Max, hopping behind the wheel. "I've got this. You can navigate." She crunched the gears as she tried to find first.

"Thank heavens they're in a box, sweetheart," Rupert quipped, as she finally found what she was looking for and roared away.

"What about your mission?" Max asked.

"All over," Rupert said, waving the gun. "Saved the world yet again. Your teachers were very helpful yesterday."

Max wondered exactly what sort of assistance they'd been able to offer and where this mission had been located, but now probably wasn't the time to ask.

Not three minutes later, two of the thugs appeared on their tail. Miss Ziegler had also managed to wrangle herself a vehicle, and Carlos, Autumn and Misha were piled in with her. The cars and scooters sped through the streets of Rome, honking and tooting, skidding and screeching. Max was glad that he'd let his sister drive as it took quite a bit of brainpower to recall all of those alleys and dead ends.

"Surely they're not going to shoot at us," Kensy said as the sound of a bullet whizzed past. It struck a flowerpot up ahead, shattering it to pieces.

Rupert chuckled. "My dear girl, I'm afraid that you and your friends have confronted the worst of the worst. The Diavolo take no prisoners, but you're right, it's terribly irresponsible of them to fire their guns in the street, particularly when I was just going to do this," he said, and leaned out of the window to take aim. There was a strange thumping sound.

Kensy looked in the rearview mirror and couldn't believe her eyes. The car behind them was enveloped in a huge bubble. Seconds later, it floated up and up and up until it disappeared beyond the rooftops. "Whoa, Mrs. Vanden Boom has been holding out on us."

"Magnificent, isn't it? Brand-spanking-new. I pre-programmed it to burst over the sewage treatment works." Rupert sat back and grinned. "Let's say they'll be seriously in the poop and we'll have some people waiting for them."

A black SUV roared out of a side street and tried to block their path. Kensy slammed on the brakes and swerved up onto the sidewalk, all the while keeping her cool.

"You're pretty good at this, Kensington, despite reducing poor Esmerelda to scrap metal. Sorry I missed Christmas, kids, but urgent business and all that. I heard that you found out about the race cars too." Rupert pouted. "It's a shame, really. I love a good surprise."

Max turned and looked at his uncle. "What race cars?"

Rupert arched an eyebrow, looking pleased. "So your sister didn't tell you. Well done, sweetheart – now I know you're good for a secret or two. They're waiting for you at Alexandria – happy Christmas, kids."

But there was no time to celebrate.

"There are Fitz and Nico!" Kensy exclaimed, spotting their scooter up ahead and the other man right on their tail. "And it's almost half past ten."

"What's Fitz doing here?" Rupert asked, sounding like a petulant child. "I thought I was the only one sent as backup."

"That way, Kens!" Max pointed to a side street coming up on their left. "It's a dead end ahead, but I'm pretty sure the scooters will get through."

The Fiat roared into the crowded piazza outside Quirinal Palace. There were protestors all over the place. Kensy honked the horn without reducing speed and people scattered. "How are we going to get inside?" she said. "The gates are closed and there are guards everywhere."

"Trust me and drive," Rupert instructed.

Kensy gulped. "But . . ."

"Do it!" Rupert ordered. "We need to be on the inside of those walls before the president and his friend leave."

With her heart in her throat, Kensy stepped on the accelerator just as the gates opened and the prime minister's Mercedes flew past into the courtyard. The car almost crashed into the president's limousine, which was on its way out. The gates began to close, but Kensy floored it, with Fitz and Nico and at least three more scooters and cars zipping through behind them. Within seconds, they were surrounded by armed men.

"Are they on our team or theirs?" Max said in confusion.

Nico leapt from the back of the scooter and ran toward his mother's car. "Mamma!"

Vittoria Vitale flung open the rear passenger door and jumped out, holding her arms wide. "Nico!" she cried, tears streaming down her face. Her husband scrambled out the other side and raced to the boy too.

The men who had been chasing them were swiftly handcuffed and arrested. But it was the sight of the president and Sergio Leonardi that was the most surprising. The president alighted from his vehicle and walked toward the prime minister.

"Primo Ministro." He leaned in to kiss her cheeks. "Whatever is happening?"

Nico kicked the man in the shins. "Mamma, the president is Diavolo and that man there," he said, pointing at Sergio, who was skulking away, "is the Head of the Devil. They have burned the farms and stolen the wheat. They wanted you to sign over Penina so they could control Italy's food supply. If you didn't, they were going to kill me. Officers, arrest them!"

The president laughed. "The boy is clearly delirious. You will not touch me."

A well-dressed man with a thick head of curly gray hair strode toward them.

"Alessandro, tell her this is a nonsense," the president cried.

Alessandro Grimaldi shook his head. "I have been waiting years for this," he said. "Thank you, Nico. You are a hero."

Kensy and Max got out of the car and were joined by Autumn, Carlos and Misha.

Alessandro Grimaldi turned to them. "I hear it is you who have helped us to bring down the most evil criminal network in Italy," he said with a smile. "I am eternally grateful."

The children stood by modestly, all except for Kensy. "Thanks," the girl said, feeling quite pleased.

"We have not yet located the woman," he said.

"You mean fake Sister Maria Regina?" Kensy said.

The man frowned. "Sister Maria Regina? But that woman is a saint."

"She's a fraud and the orphanage is a front. These men who were chasing us all work for her. She's Diavolo too," the girl replied. "The children are pickpockets and thieves and they steal the money from the Trevi Fountain."

Alessandro Grimaldi flinched. He spoke quickly into his sleeve in Italian. "*Grazie*, children. Perhaps now you will enjoy the rest of your holiday." He hurried away to speak to the prime minister.

Max turned to the others. "Is that it then?"

Autumn, Carlos and Misha nodded.

"Where's Fitz and Uncle Rupert and Miss Ziegler?" Kensy asked. She spun around, looking for them, but they had all vanished.

"What should we do with the cars?" Max asked, but it seemed they had disappeared too.

"You do realize that's our first-ever *proper* mission," Autumn said. "And we nailed it."

Carlos smiled and dusted his hands. "Yup. Mission accomplished."

"It's a shame, though, that we're not allowed to tell anyone. If we were ordinary kids and we did something like that, it would be all over the television," Misha said. "We'd be famous."

Despite having just brought down one of the worst crime syndicates in the world, Kensy and Max were both feeling a bit flat. They were no closer to finding their parents and now Fitz was gone again and they couldn't even ask him if there was any news. Their uncle was just as elusive. Being an international spy was fun, but there wasn't really anything in the way of fanfare. Talk about an anticlimax.

"Do you think you can find your way to that gelateria Mr. Frizzle promised to take us to?" Carlos asked Max. "I think we deserve a celebratory ice cream."

The boy grinned. "Sure."

The children began to walk toward the gates when they heard Nico call out to them. They turned to see him running their way.

"*Grazie!*" he said, hugging each of them.

"You rescued me from a fate I do not even want to think about, and you have saved my mother's career and the whole country from being held for ransom by the Diavolo. Mamma will be able to put an end to the wheat wars and make sure that the farmers are protected and the prices are controlled. I do not know who you really are, but I am honored to call you my friends."

The children said their goodbyes and wished the boy well.

"What about Lola?" Kensy asked as they wound their way through the streets of Rome.

Misha sighed. "She's just a kid and she's done nothing wrong, but I suspect she and her mother won't stick around for long. It's probably going to be all over the newspapers even if we're not. I'm glad I can stop acting like a mean girl at school, although I suppose I'm going to have to change slowly – it wouldn't make sense for me to be nice all of a sudden."

"Well, you can count me as your first new friend," Autumn said, linking arms with the girl. "Come on, the ice cream is on me."

CHAPTER 33

CONFESSION

Alfie looked up from his dinner as Carlos and Max slid onto the bench on the other side. "I hope you two aren't contagious."

"No, we're good now," Carlos said. "Didn't last long at all."

Alfie gave him a knowing grin as Dante and Sachin arrived at the table with their dinner.

"Well, you missed some excitement out there this afternoon. When we were on our way back from the gardens, the Trevi Fountain was closed to the public and the *carabinieri* were keeping everyone out of the piazza. We got to sneak through because Mrs. Vanden Boom said some of the children were desperate for the toilet and we should be allowed into our hotel."

"We must have still been asleep," Max said. "What happened?"

"They arrested a nun," Dante jumped in. "Can you believe it? The one in charge of the orphanage. Apparently, she'd been using the children in her care as pickpockets. It just goes to show – you never know who you can really trust."

"You can thay that again," Alfie said through a mouthful of lasagna.

Carlos and Max smiled at each other. They were pleased to hear that Sister Maria Regina had gotten her comeuppance. Surely there was a hefty penalty for impersonating a nun too – on top of her being part of the Diavolo.

"That wasn't all," Sachin added. "Lola's mother arrived and took her away. Lola was crying and stamping her feet and saying that she wanted to get her things, but her mother said there was no time and the next thing they were gone. It was weird, right?"

Carlos nodded. "Wow, so weird."

"You are going to tell us exactly what happened, aren't you?" Dante said.

Max grinned. "You'll have to wait until we're back at school. You know the rules."

* * *

Monty Reffell was glad that the unexpected excitement of the tour was over and they could get on with enjoying the rest of the trip. Today he had a full itinerary planned at the Vatican. There was a lot to see given it was its own city state, protected by the Swiss Guards in their red, blue and gold uniforms that, quite frankly, looked more like they belonged at the circus than in an army. The group had just crossed the River Tiber as he pointed out yet another church of significance along their route.

Kensy caught up to her brother, who had seemed subdued at breakfast. "Are you okay?" she asked.

"Sure," he replied, forcing a smile to his lips. "What about you?"

"Same."

Max gazed upon the river, squinting from the glare of the sun. "Don't you think it's strange that Fitz and Uncle Rupert were here yesterday and then they both just disappeared without saying a word?"

Kensy nodded. "We've only got a couple more days. Do you think . . .?"

Max looked at her. "They can't tease us like that and not show up, can they? It's worse than if we hadn't heard anything at all. At least tonight we can finally do some research about our grandparents after everyone's gone to bed."

Behind them, Romilly Vanden Boom was walking with Carlos and Autumn and catching them up on all the sights they'd missed the day before. She was very pleased to see that their fearless tour leader had decided against dressing up today and was wearing a rather stylish suit instead. It wouldn't have been a good idea to arrive at the Vatican dressed as a cardinal – that could have landed Mr. Reffell in far more trouble than his centurion outfit at the Colosseum.

As they entered St. Peter's Square, the children turned circles, in awe of the immense buildings.

"I've never seen so much marble," Inez declared. "It's breathtaking."

"Nor so many cobblestones," Harper said, glad she'd swapped her boots for sneakers that morning.

Despite it being just after half past nine there were queues upon queues of tourists. Monty Reffell took the students right around them to the group entrance of St. Peter's Basilica.

"This, my dear children, is considered to be one of the most beautiful churches in all of Christendom," Monty declared. "It's almost too magnificent to comprehend and has been known on many occasions to make grown men weep." He pulled a handkerchief from his pocket and quickly wiped his eyes.

"Are there any popes' hearts in those urns there?" Kensy asked.

"Not to my knowledge," Mr. Reffell replied, "but the tomb of St. Peter is below us in the crypt. He died at the hands of Emperor Nero, one of the most evil men to have ever ruled Rome."

"Fancy that," Autumn murmured to Kensy.

After their tour, the children were given some time to wander within a strict boundary. Monty Reffell was standing beside Alfie and Dante, staring at the mesmerizing dome painted by Michelangelo, when he felt a tap on the shoulder. A young priest spoke very quickly in Italian, but Monty didn't catch it all.

The man looked at Dante. "Moretti? What did he say?"

"He said that His Holiness is ready for you now," Dante replied.

Monty turned back to the priest. "I'm sorry, I think you have me confused with someone else."

But the fellow was insistent. Dante interpreted again, then said something to the priest, who smiled broadly and nodded his head. Monty consulted his watch. Oh, what the heck, he had half an hour before everyone was due to regroup. If the Holy Father wanted to see him, who was he to say no? The teacher felt a shiver of excitement as he scurried off with the young man. He hoped he would be allowed to take a photo or two.

"What was all that about?" Alfie asked.

Dante grinned mischievously. "The priest thinks Mr. Reffell is the president of Spain, so he's off to meet the pope."

Alfie burst out laughing, earning a sharp rebuke from one of the guards nearby. Meanwhile, on the other side of the cathedral, the real president of Spain was wondering how much longer he was going to be kept waiting. It had been an hour already.

"I feel so small in here," Kensy said to her brother, her head tilted toward the vast ceiling. They had found themselves wandering together as Autumn had gone with Harper to look at a statue she had read about. Carlos was checking out a mosaic with Sachin.

Max stopped and grabbed his sister's arm. "It's Fitz," he whispered.

Kensy turned to see the man watching them from one of the alcoves near the confessional booths. He beckoned them with the tiniest of nods. The twins hurried toward him, careful not to make a scene.

"Fitz, where have you been?" Kensy asked, hugging him fiercely. She pulled away and punched him on the arm. "We were so worried."

Fitz put a finger to his lips and pointed to one of the booths.

"Is that allowed? We've never been to confession before," Kensy said. "And what have I done wrong, anyway?"

Max looked at Fitz, their eyes locking. He took hold of his sister's hand. "Kens, just come with me," he urged. He opened the door and the pair stepped inside the dimly lit cubicle.

Max held his breath as he waited for the screen to slide open. After all that had happened, he had no idea what to expect.

"Hello, you two," a woman whispered.

"Mum?" Kensy whimpered, tears instantly pricking her eyes.

Max reached out and touched the metal screen, his forefinger pressing against his mother's on the other side. "Where have you been? Is Dad there?"

"It's too dangerous to tell you," their father replied quietly. "But we couldn't stay away any longer."

"We only have a few minutes," their mother added. "But we'll be home as soon as we can."

The children peered through the mesh although it was dark and almost impossible to see anything.

Max's mind was racing. "Why didn't you ever tell us about your life? We had no idea about any of it. And Granny – she's amazing."

"She's not bad, is she?" There was a hint of a smile in their father's voice.

"Why can't you tell us what you're looking for?" Kensy asked. "We can help. We brought down the Diavolo."

"Is it something to do with Mum's parents – the ones who were murdered?" Max added.

Their father sighed. "You've both always been too clever for your own good."

"We're putting you in terrible danger just by being here," Anna said. "We love you."

"More than you will ever know," Edward added. "Trust Fitz. He'll take care of you."

"Dad, what about Uncle Rupert? Can we trust him?" Max asked urgently.

But there was no answer. Kensy threw her arms around her brother, and the pair held each other as their tears flowed.

"Sorry," Kensy mumbled after a while. "I think I got snot on your shoulder." She pulled a tissue from her pocket and handed another to Max.

"I suppose we'd better pull ourselves together," the boy said, wiping his eyes. "It wouldn't look good for two secret agents to be caught bawling in a confessional box at the Vatican."

Kensy giggled, her eyes glistening. "True, and maybe we should leave separately. It might seem a bit weird if we go out there together."

Suddenly, their watches began to buzz, but this time it wasn't Morse code. The clockfaces disappeared, replaced by their grandmother on the screen. This was new.

"Hello, darlings," she said. "I just wanted to call and say how proud I am of you both. What you did with the Diavolo . . . Well, we've been trying to take down that lot for years."

"Thanks, Granny," the twins whispered.

"Anyway, all's well here and I can't wait to see you when you get back. Song doesn't know what to do with himself – he's been delivering scones to the whole of Ponsonby Terrace apparently," Cordelia said, chuckling.

There was a sharp knock followed by a stern voice informing them that their time was up.

"We have to go, Granny," Max said.

But when they looked at their watches there was no sign of Cordelia at all.

For the first time since their parents had gone missing, Kensy felt truly happy. "They were here," she whispered. "Right beside us."

Max squeezed his sister's hand. "And they'll be back. I know it."

THE PIGPEN CIPHER

The pigpen cipher — also known as the masonic cipher, Napoleon cipher and tic-tac-toe cipher — is a geometric simple substitution code. It exchanges letters for symbols that form fragments of a grid. Usually, the pigpen cipher alphabet is derived from the following four grids:

It is the most popular secret writing alphabet in history and has been used to encrypt all manner of things, from gravestone inscriptions to treasure maps. Don your pirate hat and consult the key below to decode the chapter headings in this book!

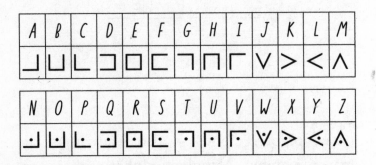

ABOUT
THE AUTHOR

Jacqueline Harvey taught for many years in girls' boarding schools. She is the author of the bestselling Alice-Miranda series and the Clementine Rose series, and was awarded Honor Book in the 2006 Australian CBC Awards for her picture book *The Sound of the Sea*. She now writes full time and is working on more Alice-Miranda, Clementine Rose, and Kensy and Max adventures.

jacquelineharvey.com.au

Read Them All!